CW00376667

T.M. Cooks is the pen name of the following collaborative writing team. The contributors are:

- Helena Holcman

- Grey Hollinrake

- Isabel O'Grady

- Sophia O'Grady

- Adam Jamil

- Evan Hughes

- Honey Bratt

- Phynn Booth

- Andreea Demian

- Zeke Griffiths

- Erin Beaven

- Ellie Pearl

The project was overseen by Joe Reddington, Dr Yvonne Skipper and Richard Seymour.

The group cheerfully acknowledges the wonderful help given by:

- Jo Rankin

- Connor Kavanagh

- Alice Bramley

- Shannon Webb

- Laura Simmons

- Amber Allcock

- Velda Jones

- Becky Walklate

- Mel Farrington

And a big thank you goes to Higher Horizons who funded this wonderful project. Its been a wonderful opportunity, and everyone involved has been filled with incredible knowledge and enthusiasm. Finally, we would like to thank all staff at Ruskin Community High School for their support in releasing our novelists from lessons for a full week.

The group started to plan out their novel at 9.15 on Monday 5 June 2023 and completed their last proofreading at 14.40 on Friday 9 June 2023.

We are incredibly proud to state that every word of the story, every idea, every chapter and yes, every mistake, is entirely their own work. No teachers, parents or other students touched a single key during this process, and we would ask readers to keep this in mind.

We are sure you will agree that this is an incredible achievement. It has been a true delight and privilege to see this group of young people turn into professional novelists in front of our very eyes.

# Project Somnium

### T. M. Cooks

# Contents

1

# Chapter 1

# Welcome To Somnium

Amongst the vibrant autumn leaves, a refreshing breeze swept softly through the air, tickling the new students on the legs. The sweet melody of birds singing a memorable tune was heard around the campus. The scent of freshly-baked cupcakes, newly-cooked pizzas and free food could be smelt. It was Fresher's Week - the end of September, a time once per year where new students arrive and feel the full force of university tradition and culture. There were people walking around in the sunshine, absorbing vitamin D into their souls, a mixture of excitement and nerves embedded deep into the atmosphere.

The front of the school looked like something out of a film. Old bricks and ancient pillars supported the memories and secrets of the many centuries that had passed. Grand, arched windows, and wide, open doors populated the walls. Places were crowded, it was as if there was a burst of energy where everyone walked. Across the huge space hundreds of student stood behind tables. "Sign up!" "Sign up!" voices were repeatedly shouting in an attempt to get new students to join their clubs, a new chance for photography, sports, art and design, even music. Students were tossing frisbees to one and other across the spacious fields. Red and purple dots scattered among the edges of the yard where blooming roses, tulips and daisies perfected the view. People were dancing about to the vibe of popular music and groovy EDM tracks. Others were telling jokes and laughing - some were telling riddles to test other students' intelligence. Some students were walking around touring or wanting tips for mental health support, tutoring or careers advice. There were stands of clubs cheering for new students to join their sports teams, political groups, movie clubs, faith organisations and social movements. It was perfect, like a dream or a fantasy, a new start to a new world. An awakening of new emotions and characteristics.

Through a large, circular window, Dr Diffshire glanced at the new students arriving. She was the type of person who had no patience for others and made them earn her respect. However, students... students were different. She had a soft spot for students, a new round of intelligence entering a certain area. Seeing all these newcomers, excited yet filled with nerves, reminded her of her days at university, a flash of nostalgia crossed her brain a few times. Diffshire was never one to speak up regularly. She was more reserved and focused on herself. Dr Diffshire knew how difficult the students' situation was. She wanted to make it perfect...

The scent of roses filled the air, as the groundskeepers strolled through the gardens.

"I love roses, " Craig proclaimed. "They're my favourite." His dog - Doug - barked as if almost in agreement.

"They're nice but I prefer tulips, they smell heavenly!" Alan stated passionately.

Alan's dog, Smudge, lay down on his back, resting. He never seemed to have any energy. Craig took a watering-can off of the ground and sprinkled the plants like glitter on paper. Alan started pulling weeds out of the ground. They both cherished the garden. Hours and hours of hard work and effort had been put into it. They didn't own it, but it felt like it was theirs, a place only they could go. A place where they were free.

A boy called Mickey leaned against a pillar, listening to his favourite song. The softness of the music made him feel warm inside, and the lyrics resonated with him. A well-dressed girl named Chanele watched him from the distance and her heart fluttered. She decided to walk up to him, but some other students got there before her: a tall boy, a brunette girl and another girl, this one short and blonde.

Chanele joined them. They were talking about what music they enjoyed the most.

"I love Lana Del Rey. I don't know if you'll have heard of her, she's kinda... underground." Chanele said.

Mickey looked at her oddly. "I'm pretty sure Lana Del Rey isn't *underground.*"

Chanele looked hurt. Nobody had ever questioned her beliefs before. She should have been angry, but this Mickey kid, he was *different.* He had a wonderful smile and he played guitar! The perfect man, Chanele thought to herself. Even though he was short, Chanele had a mental code that height wasn't really important if the person was attractive enough.

"What about you? What music do you like?" Mickey looked over towards one of the girls. Her name was Simsie. She was very short, even shorter then Mickey himself, and had short, blonde hair. She was undeniably pretty, and Chanele felt a pang of jealousy when Mickey gave her attention.

"Uh, Olivia Rodrigo? I'm not too sure."

Chanele scoffed. She knew that the blonde girl was basic, but didn't expect her to be *that* basic. She reassured herself that Mickey wouldn't fall for a girl like her. His standards weren't that low.

"Cool! What about you, Connor?"

The tall boy responded. Chanele wondered why Mickey knew his name. Maybe they went to school together? He was also very cute, but in a different way.

"I don't listen to music." Connor said, barely looking up from his sketchbook. Chanele took back her past thoughts, anyone that didn't listen to music was bound to be toxic. That was another one of her mental codes.

"Oh, okay. What about you, Paige?" Mickey pointed at the last girl, who appeared surprised. Chanele remembered her, they went to secondary school together and used to be friends. She wasn't as cute as Simsie, she gave off a more tomboy-ish vibe with her shaggy hair and casual outfit.

"I like Harry Styles. He's really good at singing, you know."

Chanele was surprised. She assumed that Paige wouldn't listen to something that popular. "Cool. What about you, Mickey?" She asked, batting her eyelashes at him.

"Not sure. I listen to loads of stuff." He replied, putting books into his backpack.

As they were talking, a lecturer strolled beside them and decided to give her opinions on the matter. "I love Pulp, personally. But you wouldn't have heard of them." She looked at the students hopefully, hoping that they would've heard of the unknown music she enjoyed.

"Yeah, you're right. Never heard of them." Chanele said.

The poor lecturer walked away, disappointed with Chanele's rudeness. She stepped on crunchy, autumnal leaves as the students spoke, making her way towards the main building of Somnium University.

# Chapter 2

# Chanele's Nightmare

Chanele crawled into her bed, adorned with linen sheets and sleek plush pillows. She'd heard once that your bedroom is a reflection of your mind, so she made sure to decorate her sleeping space in the most expensive finds. Designer coffee table books were scattered on her desk, organised to look messy enough so that it looked effortless, but neat enough so that it was still tidy. *Effortless beauty*, she called it, and strove to embody those two words in her every action, thought process, gesture, and mere existence really. If she gave up on being pretty she wouldn't know how to be alive.

That's why she'd refused all snacks offered to her throughout the day. With the desire to be perfect came the desire to be thin, and being thin meant enduring the hunger a little bit longer. If she managed to go so long without eating, why stop now? Tomorrow was a new day, a brand new set of 24 hours for her to deny her body the disgusting "pleasure" of indulging in a fattening meal, and instead granting herself the privilege of malnourishment, of being light and dainty.

Right now though, her limbs felt heavy, weary from the long day. She let herself drift off to sleep, as there's no point in being small if your dark circles are humongous. Not that she minded - it made her look fierce in a Bella Hadid kind of way, and even her eyebags were designer.

When she woke up the next morning, she instinctually reached down to feel her ribcage, making sure she could still count each bone, only to realise they weren't there. Weird. She was at least 98 lbs, 100 maximum - there's no way she could've gained more than 2 lbs overnight. Body checking had become a subconscious part of her routine, so she only realised she was doing it when her body didn't feel the way she'd expected it to. She propped herself up onto both elbows, occurring to her then that she was staring at the body of her 10 year old self. Of course! At 10 her BMI was double her age, a pathetic number compared to such a remarkable girl who possessed so much potential.

Her self-absorbed train of thought was abruptly interrupted when she heard yelling downstairs, a man and a woman. Her parents.

Oh.

She was back in her childhood bedroom, as her 10 year old self, in a house whose walls felt suffocating. She felt trapped, vulnerable. That was bad - vulnerability led to getting hurt. At least she wasn't the one suffering yet, though.

Mother's shriek echoed through the house, the sound of hands on skin, then a thud. She was unconscious, she was sure - her father wasn't a weak hitter. But her mother wasn't a weak woman, she would fight back to protect her daughter. Right? Chanele didn't want to find out, and she knew better than to investigate.

As she pulled the covers over her head, feeling slightly more safe cloaked in her blanket of safety, she heard stomping up the stairs.

*Oh.*

Her father was approaching her room. That wasn't good, that was never good. The way he walked so aggressively made it seem like each step was an effort to intimidate her into a position of fear, where she was easier to keep in line. *Please, not now, not again.*

The door swung open, the doorknob making an indent in the wall, and suddenly a beam of light shone on her face.

Chanele sat up, dishevelled, breathing erratically. She'd forgotten to close her blinds last night, allowing for the sun's glow to land right on her sweet face at the crack of dawn. Oh. It was a bad dream. Weird, she couldn't recall any memories of her family, or even having one in the first place. Maybe it was a metaphor for something? Whatever, no time to think now.

Despite it being 5:30 am she had overslept, and needed to get ready for the day.

She got up and turned on the shower. Her morning routine lasted only 2 hours, after narrowing it down due to not having enough storage in her tiny dorm bathroom to cram all of her expensive products in. Stepping on to the cold shower tile, her stomach rumbled, reminding her of what she would have to put up with today. Whatever - it was worth it if it meant she could stay thin.

# Chapter 3

# The First Meal

Students scurried into the bright cafeteria, eager to try one of Will's famous homemade croissants. There was a moment of admiration as the freshers looked around the hall. It smelt of warm pastries and the sun trickled down through the windows, shining onto the students faces.

Will stood in delight at the entrance, holding out his baking tray, telling the students to take a pastry.

"One per person, " Will said demandingly, swatting away students trying to get seconds. One by one, his delicacies disappeared from the hot tray and into the cradling hands of eager students.

Paige walked past Will, taking a croissant,

"Thanks sir, " she said happily.

"You're very welcome!" Will replied, flashing Paige a warm smile. He offered one of his treats to Chanele but she walked past him, tense and shook from her nightmare the previous evening. *That's strange*, Will thought to himself as he looked back to the horde of oncoming students.

Abruptly, there was a loud crash.

"Great, " Will mumbled under his breath. Suddenly, Mickey and Connor came rushing into the cafeteria. They walked past Will, snatching a croissant each.

"Cheers, sir!" Mickey yelled back at Will as he walked off.

"You're welcome, " Will said back to him, sarcastically. Paige and Chanele sat down . Paige took a bite out of her croissant as she looked over to see Chanele, once again distraught and pale.

"Are you okay?" Paige asked quietly, "Chanele?" she asked again, looking at her friend.

"What?" Chanele snapped, taken by surprise and seemingly annoyed.

"What are you looking at?"

"Nothing." Chanele said plainly. Paige followed her gaze, certain she was hiding something.

"You were looking at Mickey weren't you?" Paige said, gasping.

"I was not!" Chanele hissed, her face reddening.

"Sure you weren't." Paige replied sarcastically, letting out a quiet laugh.

Will was still stood by the doors. He watched as the last few students walked through the entrance politely taking the last of his pastries. His eyes scanned across the room and noticed Chanele staring at Mickey with eyes wide like cherry pies. *Yo-*

*ung love* Will thought as he remembered his youth. He walked back to the kitchen thinking about his little boy Mark. He had seen him last week but it felt like a lifetime since they had been together. He gently closed the door behind him placing the baking tray down to his side. Will rubbed his forehead faintly before going to wash the dishes he had dirtied.

Will turned on the taps before adding dish soap to the sink. The water was hot and fogged up his glasses. He took them off before wiping the lenses with a cloth. Once he put his glasses back on he noticed one croissant left on the baking tray. He walked over to it taking a long look at it.

He looked around carefully for a moment before taking a bite. His face felt warm as he swallowed it. *Perfect* he thought to himself before continuing to eat the rest of the savoury snack.

# Chapter 4

# Lancaster's Lecture

A crisp breeze ran through the hallway, cooling everything with its touch. It was only late September, yet the weather had already begun to deteriorate. The new students were lined up outside Miss Lancaster's lecture hall, some of them shivering, all eagerly talking to each other about what might happen once they were in the room.

"She'll probably just talk to us about what it'll be like after this week, " remarked Connor.

"Maybe she'll tell us about where all the rooms are. I nearly got lost on my way over here, " complained Chanele, flicking her blonde hair dramatically to the side.

"No, she won't tell us that. We'll find out about that later, in that speech we're supposed to have after this, " Simsie corrected.

"Good morning everyone, "

The students all turned around to find Miss Lancaster waving and smiling enthusiastically in their direction. Slightly scared, but still excited, the students quickly filed into the hall.

Once everyone had settled in their seats (it took a while to do so, as the room was quite confined) Miss Lancaster began her talk.

"Hello, my name is Miss Lancaster, I won't bother with introductions for now, but I shall hopefully learn all of your names in time. So, I am sure that you are all very eager to find out what you will be doing this week, but I shall not reveal anything yet, as you will learn all that you need to know in the speech that your Vice Chancellor, Dr Diffshire, will be presenting to you soon in the main lecture hall, " She paused for a brief moment to rearrange some papers on her desk "Now, I will not keep you waiting, but there are some things I wish address before you go. Firstly, you probably already know that after this week you will be in normal lectures, and that all the festivities occurring at the present moment will cease. However, this does not mean that your time here will not be exciting, especially not in my literature lessons..." She carried on talking about the coming week, what they would learn, what they would do, and was successful in putting most of the class to sleep.

After what seemed like hours, Miss Lancaster stopped for a moment and picked up the pile of papers that she had rearranged during her speech.

"Right, here are some posters which hold information concerning the societies you can join here. Mickey Griffiths?, " she paused, worried that she might have addressed the wrong student.

"Yes Miss?" he replied.

She breathed a sigh of relief "Could you please hand these out?" she said, holding out the posters towards him. He ungracefully stepped out from his row, knocked against some students along the way, managed to stumble up to Miss Lancaster, and took the papers from her.

He began to hand them out, but once he had got to middle row, he thought it would be better to try and reach over to the row above to speed up the process. However, he struggled due to the limitations of his height. As he did so, Chanele looked over in his direction, and stared at him for quite some time. Afraid that someone noticed, she turned her head away, her cheeks flushed a deep shade of red.

Once a few minutes had elapsed, Mickey sat down in his row, and the other students picked up the posters and studied their contents.

"I can't believe they don't have a tennis society!" Simsie grumbled.

"Oh look! They have an Art and Design club." exclaimed Chanele.

"Indeed." whispered Connor, who began to study the information about the club.

"I'll join the literature society." mentioned Paige.

Suddenly, a bell rang, different than the one that had signalled breakfast, its violent voice bleeding into every corner of the room. As the students finished off writing a few notes concerning the lecture, they began to vacate the room, chattering noisily along the way.

"Don't forget about the speech, " Miss Lancaster mentioned "You won't want to miss it!"

# Chapter 5

# Diffshire's Dialogue

The main lecture theatre appeared to be quite aged, with an archaic atmosphere hanging around its structure. All the students were now seated in the rows, an excited murmur scurried from one to the other like a plague. Unexpectedly, a figure materialised from the shadows in the corner of the room, and began to stride over to the podium at the front of the hall. Once the figure had emerged upon the stage and departed from the shadows, all the features became clear. It was a woman, no older than thirty, dressed in a paper white, long-sleeve shirt, a well fitting beige blazer with a matching knee length skirt and a pair of brown stilettos which were pointed at the tips. She had a soft face with a pale complexion (bright blue eyes the colour of a clear sky, a small button-like nose, thin eyebrows that resembled twigs and lips as thin as paper), and blonde, waist length hair that draped over her head like a silk table cloth.

Be that as it may, her posture was stiff and awkward, she had an uneasy smile, and she appeared to be trembling, which gave her the appearance of an image glitching on a screen.

"Go-G-Goodmo-Goodmorning eve-everyone, " she stopped abruptly to fidget nervously with her hands as she noticed that all the students had now turned their attention to her "I'm Dr-Dr Diff-Diffshire, t-tha-thank you for joining Somnium University."

She readjusted her posture and now stood a few centimetres taller than she did before. "Today I shall be introducing you to all the events that shall occur over the duration of this week, and what will happen in the wake of these experiences. I would begin with the information about the clubs and where your dorms are, but I have asked your lecturers to tell you all the information about the societies beforehand, and you have already spent the night here, " She paused to take a piece of lint off her shoulder "Now, this week, there will be absolutely no lectures, there will only be meetings with your lecturers and teachers to explain all the details of next week furthermore. Instead, there will be barbecues, events, parties, live music and food in the student union. There is no need to pay for anything, it's all free, especially the food..." Connor and Mickey look at each other.

"Why does she keep on mentioning food?" Connor questioned.

Mickey shrugged "Don't know."

They both turn back to Dr Diffshire (who was talking about the layout of the campus) "...The campus was built and designed in the 13th century, but has been renovated quite a few times since, and the gardens were created in the 19th century, 1810, to be exact. But I will not bore you with all of these details that might seem inconvenient to you. You will have noticed that there was a piece of paper on your chairs before, " she pauses as the students took pieces of paper out from under their chairs. "These are maps of Somnium, they will aid you when you are lost. But you must at the least know where the cafeteria is, " as she said this she stared intently at each and every student, like a hawk scanning the landscape for prey.

After an unusually awkward silence Dr Diffshire stepped off the podium, the old wood panels creaking in protest under her steps and dismissed the students with a wave of the hand, like a queen would dismiss her subjects.

But before any one had properly exited their rows, Dr Diffshire had shouted "Wait!" Everyone turned around, perplexed as to what she might want to add that was so important.

"You must, " she said "Attend each breakfast, every lunch, and every single dinner. You must not miss *any*, no matter what!"

# Chapter 6

# Alarming Times

After Dr Diffshire finished her speech,

the students filed into a corridor, discussing what they had just been told. Fresher's Week had only just started, yet all the students had so much work to do, so much to remember. Eventually they dispersed, running off to different activities being held on campus.

Suddenly, an ear piercing alarm rang, causing all of them to shudder. Panic spread across the campus. People screamed, people ran and a particularly nervous fresher tucked herself into a ball, crying for her life. The corridors were demented, people stampeding over others.

Craig shouted over the noise, trying to calm the students, "It's time for lunch, let's go!" Alan nodded and they both began to walk to the cafeteria. As Alan and Craig hurried to the cafeteria, the students followed, feeling reasonably less hysterical. The wailing siren grew louder, letting everyone in the university know it was time to eat.

Connor stopped drawing, his still image of the university gardens unfreezing as he shoved his sketchbook into his backpack. He rose from his seat, a twisting oak tree, and made his way to the cafeteria, his tall frame being untouched by the ecstatic fresher beside him.

Simsie Brown dropped her tennis racket, missing the match point against a competitive senior. She drowsily sighed, grabbing her woollen tote bag from the corner of the court. The senior walked past her and laughed, patting the top of her head like a dog. Simsie glared at him and stormed off to lunch, feeling disappointed in herself.

Paige closed her book, *Sense And Sensibility*, and got up too, glancing at Connor from the corner of her eye. All of them knew what the alarm sounded like, so they knew where to go. Students frantically made their way towards the cafeteria, eager to eat Will's appetising food. They had to be on time; if you were late, you faced extreme punishment.

People were running, including Chanele. She was more of a "walk and talk" kind of girl, but even she didn't want to face any punctuality consequences. Unfortunately for her (and her pride) Chanele tripped and fell to the floor. You would think everyone would have stopped to look at her but they didn't. Nobody did, even though deep down she hoped at least one person would pay attention to her (then again maybe it was better they didn't, as it would save her the humiliating conversation). Everyone was too focused on getting there on time. If you were to look around you would think there was a murderer on the loose.

The double glass doors were already propped open, waiting for the swarm of famished freshers. The racket of the students grew louder and louder as they came closer and closer. Suddenly, the uproar ended when Dr Diffshire appeared. She stood in the doorway, hands on her hips, lips sealed, waiting for silence. As she stepped aside she announced "Enter." It took only two minutes until everyone was stood in the cafeteria searching for their designated seat.

Some students groaned about the assigned seating, wanting to be sat next to their friends, wanting to be moved, but Dr Diffshire shot them a cut-throat stare and they miraculously quietened.

Once everyone was seated, the room remained silent, apart from the occasional breaths from the nervous freshers. No one was shouting, no one was smiling. In fact, no one looked happy at all.

A whiff of freshly baked bread drifted through the air, causing smiles to be exchanged to one another. Chanele was sat on her seat, staring at the shiny, metal door whilst fixing her hair in the reflection. Then, as if to purposefully ruin her day, the kitchen door flung open, trapping her between it and the wall. A warm draft of air passed her, dishevelling her painstakingly perfect hair.

Mr Dutton, or Will, the dinner man, walked out of the kitchen with a big silver trolley filled with delectable food. The students glared at the trolley, watching it roll past each table, waiting for it to be their turn. No one was sat still, legs were twitching, hands couldn't be kept stable, they were all so exhilarated to get their food.

After everyone had settled down they were finally allowed to eat their food. All the new students began to eat. Dr Diffshire surveyed the room, scanning each student at every table to make sure they were eating everything.

They all did, scoffing up every last crumb, begging Will for seconds. Dr Diffshire smiled, happy that all the students were staying well-nourished.

That was, everyone except Chanele. She watched Diffshire intently, waiting until she was on the other side of the room. If the faculty members of this university wanted to ruin her hair, fine. She would make no effort to eat what they served her, completely disregarding the care they put into making sure each student had a warm meal to eat. Those miserable pigs, stuffing their mouths up until their stomachs were packed full.

Why they chose temporary satisfaction over long term results, she had no idea. *Food lasts a second, skinny lasts a life-time.* She'd come up with many similar sayings and phrases to encourage her eating disorder, and it worked. That's not to say that she had no appetite; food was all she could think about, besides her gorgeous face. She was obsessed with food: nutritional information - macronutrients, micronutrients - planning her next meal and making sure it met her protein goal and carb limit for the day, all whilst falling within her calorie limit. Obsession was unhealthy though, and a woman stressing too much led to her getting wrinkles, meaning Chanele could either become focused on food *and* save up for botox, or ignore it all together. She chose the latter.

As she sat there, making small talk with her schoolmates at the table, she could see the growing concern on their faces when they stared at her still-full plate. If suspicion arose around her eating habits, her plan would come to an untimely end. That couldn't happen. It *wouldn't.* Musing over her options in that situation, an idea struck her. Whilst she couldn't chew and spit in public, and it was hard to pretend that you ate with the Vice Counsellor scanning the room like a hawk, she could hide the fact she was pretending.

Waiting for her opportunity, she took a handful of the garden salad on her plate and stuffed her pockets. Thank god she wasn't wearing expensive jeans, otherwise that would be four figures down the drain. Tomato juice soaked into the denim, coating her thigh in that nasty fluid that comes out when you slice tomatoes. In that moment she wished, like every other woman before her wished at least once in their life, that woman's jeans came with bigger pockets.

Her next victim was the pork sausage sat haphazardly amongst her vegetables.

The thing was fried in so much oil that it was enough to rival the greasy hair of a sweaty fourteen year old boy who swears he showers every day, when in reality it's more like once a month. There was no way *that* was going anywhere near her clothes. Changing her expression from one of revolt to one of mild aversion, she locked eyes with one of the students at her table and said, "Hey, do you mind eating this for me? I'm vegetarian, so I can't have meat." Chanele made sure to smile politely for added effect.

The girl-she-didn't-care-enough-about-to-remember-her-name fell for it. "Um...sure. I don't mind. Wait, how did you finish your food already?"

"I just scoffed it down, I was so hungry. Thanks by the way, you're the best!"

as she slid the oleaginous thing onto the other's plate, she made a mental note to not eat any meat from now on, at least around the girl she just spoke to, so as to preserve the lie of her being a vegetarian. Not a lie she wanted to fall into - it came with annoying restrictions, such as not being able to consume chicken as a protein source - but the advantage of being able to refuse certain foods was worth it.

That jarring bell rang again, signalling the end of lunch time. As students walked out, Chanele sought to find Paige, calling Mr. Dutton some not-so-nice things in her head when she passed him because he ruined her fabulous hairstyle.

# Chapter 7

# John Mcrawler

NOTES:

My name is John Mcrawler and I'm the CCTV or technician of the university. In front of me was a white, shiny desk with a spin-type office chair. Resting on the table was a modern keyboard and mouse with a mobile to the left of the keyboard. Surrounding the keypad were three computers, two angled slightly in. On one computer screen led a coding app, the other a CCTV checker for close up sight and the last a black screen. This is what I use for work. Behind the computers was a huge screen of individual CCTV cameras of random pinpoint locations across the university.

I heard a angry drum beat coming from the floorboards outside. I continued coding and doing other CCTV nonsense. Next minute I hear a loud banging sound coming off the door. Through the rectangular glass in the upper centre of the door, white wire mesh in diamond shapes cutting through the glass like a knife.

As Dr Diffshire walked in, it sounded like an elephant horde rushed through the door. The stomp of her heels made a thud of thunderclouds rumbling in the sky.

She walked in with a troubling look in her eyes, clearly she wanted a serious conversation, I'm guessing about the students.

She was talking about each individual student, she said, "The first student is called Connor, he is a taller boy, quite smart, no scars or birthmarks, brunette hair. The next is Paige, dark hazel hair, brown eyes, she's making quite a lot of friends so far and her fashion choice is towards the lavish side, her fears include loneliness, dark places and a few others. Then Simsie, she has dirty blond hair and grey eyes, she's a tennis prodigy and very shy. Her fears include enclosed spaces and loss of control. The next is Chanele. She's 19 years old. She has flaxen coloured hair; she has brown eyes; she's 5'8", she's thin, good-looking, she used to have a nose-piercing. I don't know if she still does though. Her fears include her looks and losing attractiveness. The next is Mickey; who has black hair, green eyes, his fear is falling out with family".

I wasn't ignoring her but I just turned back to get on with some work because you never know if I could miss something on the CCTV cams or accidentally delete some vital coding.

I suddenly got a buzzing sound coming from the left of the table. The phone was ringing. I slowly picked it up to hear the security guard on the other side. He wanted to check on the security protocols, asking question like are the cameras picking up on things? Are we doing enough if there is an emergency? As I was on the phone I could distinctly still make out the ruffling of Dr Diffshire's voice still talking about the students and how good their progress is coming along so far.

After a while of talking about the students, she suddenly started talking about the food in the canteen. I explained to the security guard as an excuse that I'm really busy and Dr Diffshire has strict orders to give me. I hung up after finishing the chat with the security guard and then had a leisurely discussion on the food, discussing if we are giving these students enough food breaks and no mishaps are occurring.

Question after question, it started to sound like someone was booking times for a holiday. I asked, "How much food are we giving these bright students you say?" She replied with, "Three courses a day with two snack breaks over the day."

I instantly exclaimed, " Do you think that's enough or should we have more?" She didn't reply to that question. Probably thinking about the extra drugs needed taken or if any nurses can advance the drug without advancing the side effects like drowsiness or headaches.

# Chapter 8

# Speechless

Paige and Connor floated through the

long, winding corridors, engaging in mindless conversations. They turned a corner and bumped into a short, slim figure, shying away from them like an introvert. Paige kept quiet but Connor spoke up, having seen the familiar figure before.

"Hey! Simsie, right?" He called out to the girl. She snapped her head around, seemingly surprised that someone said her name. She was used to shying away, being invisible to the crowd whatever the situation. It was a rare occasion that somebody payed her any attention, let alone shouting out her name in a university corridor of all places.

"Yeah." She whispered in a timid way. "Nice to meet you."

The three students chatted some more, about courses, professors, and activities.

They came across a small vending machine, filled with a variety of treats from chocolates to sweets - vending machines were scattered all around campus supplying fresh treats to students - and they decided to buy a snack each. Paige slotted in 3 pound coins and they were soon all given their favourite sugary snacks. She and Connor opened theirs and started eating right away, whereas Simsie slipped hers into her jacket pocket for later.

"Do you know Chanele?" Connor asked, a mouthful of chocolate and a hint of suspicion in his voice. He looked around cautiously, as if she was there, listening in to their conversation like a member of the CIA or FBI on a secret mission.

"Yeah, why?" Simsie questioned. She knew Chanele, she had seen her around before but they had never really talked. She wondered what she had done, what dirt was on her.

"Apparently she's been having all these weird nightmares. She's saying she's hallucinating and seeing herself in an asylum with a hospital gown."

Paige looked peeved, an unhappy expression forming on her face. "Not *just* Chanele. Other people see things too. Don't put the blame on her."

Connor replied instantaneously, " I'm not putting the blame on her, I'm just saying that it's strange that it's happening."

Simsie went to speak, but suddenly her voice croaked like a frog and she fell silent, making gasping noises. Her heart started thumping in her chest, desperately trying to use her frozen vocals chords. The more she tried speaking, she could feel like she was mouthing words but nothing was coming out of her shy, introverted mouth. Although this had never happened before, Simsie found an ounce of familiarity in her voice being silenced.

Paige jumped up and slapped her hard on the back. "Are you choking?" Simsie spluttered, shaking her head furiously. Connor dragged the overreacting girl off her and reassured her that Simsie was joking, laughing at her foolishness.

"Very funny, Simsie."

She smiled at them, not wanting to explain that she physically couldn't speak. She thought on telling them it was sort of a panic attack 'thing' about her. She took the chocolate bar out of her pocket and started eating it, nodding whilst Paige and

Connor spoke to each other. Suddenly, the tightness in her throat dispersed and she spoke again, feeling so, so, so grateful.

An awkwardness in her tone, Simsie giggled, backing away slowly. "Sorry, I have to go. I need to um... feed my fish!"

She darted away, trying not to make eye contact with the two students. How embarrassing...

# Chapter 9

# Remember The Roses

Craig and his dog (Doug) and Alan and his dog (Smudge) were standing next to a pretty red brick building where students were busy meeting new people and signing up for clubs.

"Have you done the grass yet?" Craig asked Alan pointing towards the bright field behind the lively students.

"Yeah, all done, " Alan continued whilst bending down to fuss Smudge, "don't worry about it."

"Okay, good." Craig smiled and gave Doug a treat, "So, how you been?"

"Good but I miss my old friends, a lot actually." Alan felt a little down and lonely after working for so long. Craig patted him on the back and the pair began walking toward the messy, unattended bushes lining the gate. Smudge was taking bites out of plants until Alan shouted at him. Craig grabbed his purple shears out his old dirty bag and was about to begin. Doug began barking and yapping at the edge of campus, like he saw something. Alan dazed out over the bushes, "Hey, I can't remember what it's like outside here..."

"Wait. I don't know either." Craig replied, confused.

Alan and Craig were still trying to remember; they both couldn't understand why they didn't know. Doug and Smudge barked and barked at the the gate, however, there was nothing there. Alan and Craig looked at the two dogs, wondering what they were so angry about. Craig looked out the rusty gate to see if there was maybe something there. He could no longer think - he went a little dizzy and stumbled, then snapped back sharply and said in a forceful voice, "We need to prune the roses." Alan didn't find it strange and agreed, they walked off taking their garden supplies with them. Doug was running alongside the fast paced groundskeepers. Smudge was panting and barely keeping up.

They walked over the vibrant pathways towards the old wooden tool shed to get the supplies needed to freshen the roses near Miss Lancaster's arched window. Craig reached for his watering can from the higher shelf, he couldn't manage to get it as there was too many boxes in the way. Bringing his hand down, his sleeve got caught on a nail and he fell, ripping his worn jacket. "Oh no, this was my favourite jacket." Craig groaned as he stood up, "I'll go and get another one, I'll be back!"

As he was leaving, Alan watched Doug run after him, wondering if someone ever would love him as much as Craig loved Doug. Alan had always been lonely, he had no family, not any that he talked to anyway. Except from Smudge. Even though he was a dog, Smudge was basically family. Despite his furry friend, Alan still longed for someone to be with, to love. Whilst Craig was gone, he got down the watering cans and pruners for the roses. "You're back! Nice jacket." he said as he passed Craig his watering can.

Alan gazed at Craig as he walked away holding Doug's leash, he smiled to himself. Craig quickly turned and asked "You coming?" Alan nodded and followed him to the messy roses that were desperately in need of sorting. Smudge was jogging behind, trying to keep up. "C'mon Doug!" He yelled at his dog, who was staring into somebody's bedroom window and barking in a crazy manner.

# Chapter 10

# Forget The Freedom

NOTES:

I sometimes hate my job, just sitting in a chair all day, practically gamer-necking all the time to the point where I'm in a perpetual state of neck pain. I have to put up with it though because this profession pays really well - almost 60, 000 a year.

Out of nowhere, on one of the screens, I saw two people, who looked like gardeners. They were inspecting the plants to see if any needed to be improved. I overheard Diffshire saying that they do a really good job but most of the time the students pay no attention to the work they do, it's as if they didn't exist in the university at all. I noticed a dog on one side of Alan. Alan's dog is a huge, fat, fluffy Labrador. Meanwhile the other guy, Craig, has a small sausage dog with so much energy that Craig has to call out just to keep it from running too far away.

I'm fed up of this CCTV nonsense, I just sit there and if anything suspicious happens, I code a couple lines and sound an alarm for security. Utterly disappointing. I raised my fist in rage and banged down on the desk a few times, objects on the table leaping a few centimetres in any direction. I could feel my blood boil in anger. I wanted something else to do than sit in this throne of lies.

My fingers started moving swiftly typing what I actually can do well. My fingers were moving so fast, it looked like a blur. My fingers gliding across the keyboard.

As Craig and Alan walked up to the rusted gate, it was grand and brown, standing around 10 metres tall. It is combined with beige-brown brick pillars either side. On the pillars, the bottom half was a dark brown brick separated by a beige brick on the upper. These pillars both support either side. The main gate itself had a rectangular main shape with a semi-circular top. On top of the gates hold long metal spikes preventing unneeded regular people strolling into the university. Towards the left of the gate lay a patch of tulips and rose bushes. Surrounding over the top and sides led a leafy hedge with a little patch of leaves towards the bottom left corner of the gate that if you walked through it would probably tickle your legs. However, on the right side, grew poison ivy stretching across and upwards in random directions, nature's weapon separating. Alan looked at Craig and judging by his face, they both felt a huge temptation to cut or remove the ivy.

"Doug, fetch me my clippers please, " Craig commanded. I started typing again on my keyboard on a new tab on the black coding screen and implants into the algorithm a memory of a task to do that was set this morning. The tiny dachshund scurried away to retrieve the equipment. Smudge followed behind, panting and attempting to keep up.

"Don't worry, " Alan responded telling Smudge and Doug to return, "We can do that later, I've heard from a gardening student that there was weeds and ivy starting to grow near the front of the school." They started to ponder in the direction of the school front attempting to find the location of the vile plants.

As they approached the parched plants, Doug and smudge were both sat waiting patiently for them. The tools that Craig had asked for were laid in front of them, covered in warm, slimy dog saliva. "How did you two know that we were going to be here?" Alan questioned. Doug and Smudge stared at them with blank expressions. "I told you Doug was smart!" Craig insisted. "Smudge must've followed him here."

"No, Smudge is clearly the smart one! Doug is the dumb one who runs into doors and chases bees."

After around fifteen minutes of regular gardening, they started discussing life, I noticed that they were talking about friends outside the campus. I could see them on my screen, I zoomed into that camera footage. I stared at them intently, *what were they up to?* I saw that they were looking over the gate, it was my time, my time to do my job. I turned my head to my coding screen and typed code. I could then see that they had walked away.

# Chapter 11

# Lancaster's Love

Click. Clack. Click. Clack. The sounds

of keys being pressed by Miss Lancaster was almost like a rhythm. She was writing about Jacobean poetry. It came easy to her. She understood it so well that she did not need to stop typing and think about it. She was amazed by each and every word and found a deeper meaning from each line. She loved it... almost as much as she loved Craig, the quiet groundskeeper. She was in awe of how he acted, how he spoke, how he dressed.

Nothing could make her lose focus. Nothing could take her mind away from her favourite love sonnets.

WOOF! WOOF! The sound frightened her for a second as she jumped up.

Peering out of her window, she noticed Craig trimming the hedges with his dog aggressively barking at a bee. He payed extreme attention to fine details. Everything he did had to be perfect. That is why she could not mess this up. But how would she start a conversation? Would she whistle a tune to get his attention? Would she start to laugh at his dog attacking the bee? Either way, it would have to be perfect.

"I used to have a dog, " Miss Lancaster shouted down. "His name was Wispa."

"That's a wonderful name!" Craig replied. "What type of dog was he?"

"He was a Westipoo, " Miss Lancaster answered. "His fur was brown like chocolate so I named him after my favourite chocolate bar - a Wispa!"

"Aw, that's nice." Craig stated. "Doug got his name from me misspelling dog!"

Miss Lancaster laughed. "Well it certainly suits him." she responded.

"He loves helping me out with my work!. Or just getting in the way!" Craig laughed.

"Well you certainly seem to do a good job, " Miss Lancaster claimed. "I could never garden. I'm not very good with my hands but, it seems really fun!"

"It is, " Craig proclaimed, "I love it. My mother taught it to me at a young age and it became my passion. After she passed, it felt like a duty to keep her garden looking magnificent. She is the reason I've gone down this career path."

"That's really sweet, " Miss Lancaster replied. "You must really like nature then."

"Yes, it can be so calm and relaxing!" Craig added.

This was her chance now. Her chance to get him to come inside and finally ask him out. But what if he didn't want to. Could he even come inside? After all, he was working. And *would he even want to*? He loved his gardening and he wouldn't stop just for an English lecturer. Would he? "Not many people seem to notice my gardening, " Craig replied. "I don't really mind though. As long as I'm happy with it, then it doesn't matter!"

"I certainly noticed it. I find it wonderful." Miss Lancaster smiled.

"Thanks, " Craig smiled back.

"Well I've got to go now. I need to uh... do this thing somewhere else." Craig lied.

"Oh. Okay then. I'll see you around then." Miss Lancaster replied, with a hint of sadness in her tone. She sounded almost hurt.

"Yeah, I'll see you around" Craig said

as he hurried off. Doug followed him, panting and holding a pair of his hedge clippers in his mouth.

Miss Lancaster placed her laptop on her desk. Made of oak and painted crimson, her desk had virtually everything she could have possibly needed. Pens, pencils, paper, tissues, sharpeners - she had it all. It was organised very particularly. Nothing could be out of place. It reflected her personality. She turned round and went to sit down.

A body, laying down on her chair - it was the corpse of a man in his fifties. There was no life in him. *He looked scared.* In an old-fashioned jacket with buttons missing, a stain covered his chest. A sea of deep red, dripping down his stiff body. Miss Lancaster seemed to know him, yet she couldn't put a name to the face. The cold, lifeless face.

She rubbed her eyes. It was gone. No more dead corpse on her chair. No more blood dripping on her carpet. No more trouble. What had happened? Was it real? Was she seeing things? After all, she only got a couple hours of sleep last night. Was she going crazy? Questions filled her head and she needed a solution. Chocolate. Food always seemed to make everything okay. Fortunately, she had a pack of Wispas in her desk. Her favourite. Scurrying over, she was shaking. Sweat began to slowly trickle down her cheek. Opening her desk's draw, she took out a chocolate bar in a purple wrapper. She opened it and swiftly took a bite. Then another. And another. Throwing the wrapper in a bin, she sat back down at the desk and picked up her laptop. She began to write. Click. Clack. Click. Clack.

# Chapter 12

# Sinners Play as Saints

Out of the corner of her eye, Chanele noticed Mickey sitting on one of the campus' wooden benches, all by himself. He twisted the tuners of his guitar, strumming it occasionally. Chanele looked at the young boy, sitting all by himself and felt confident. She knew that if she wanted to make a move on him, she'd have to do it now. There's no way he wouldn't be charmed by her irresistible demeanour, she was sure.

"Hey, Mickey!" she announced, tucking a strand of her blonde hair behind her ear. Mickey was taken aback, while she was one to initiate conversation, she wasn't one to take an interest in other people.

"Hi Chanele, how are you?" he responded, scanning her confident, slightly flustered expression. Chanele took a deep breath, eager to discuss the events that had happened in her life. She could talk about herself for hours. If it was a competitive sport, she would be in first place, and not just because she's the best at everything, either.

"I'm doing great, actually. It was my friend's birthday yesterday. We went to this fancy restaurant and got drunk off top-shelf liquor. Then we went to the planetarium - we had to hitch-hike since we couldn't drive, we blasted music with the windows rolled down - and we were watching all the galaxies whilst buzzed out of our minds. It was such a vibe. I kept seeing kaleidoscopic patterns for like hours after. But then I had to come back to school. It's alright I guess, mainly boring though. Did

I tell you I'm an aspiring model? I don't get why I have to learn all this, surely my flawless face would be enough to get me a contract with an agency. I like Miss Lancaster's class the best though. That speech she gave kind of freaked me out." She spewed out every word that was on her mind, stringing them together into barely-coherent sentences, like beat poetry on amphetamines.

Mickey smiled politely. "That's great, Chanele." It was then realised her misstep - not mistake because she doesn't make mistakes, just happy accidents - she had blabbered on about herself for too long, to the point were Mickey didn't seem too engaged in the conversation. She decided to shut up, shifting the focus from her to him. He wasn't instantly interested in her, that was fine. She'd just let him talk about himself instead, pretending to be interested in whatever he had to say. It would make him feel important, stroke his ego, and he'd want to spend more time with her. Who wouldn't want to spend more time with someone who made them feel special? She needed something else to talk about.

There it was! She noticed a stack of music sheets tucked away in his backpack and decided to strike up a conversation again. If she had learned one thing in her 19 years on Earth, it was that people loved talking about themselves.

"Music sheets? They look cool, do you write your own?"

Mickey looked surprised, why was Chanele being so nice? He felt really confused, but still decided to answer. Maybe she was changing for the best?

"Uh, sure? What do you want to hear?"

Chanele grabbed the sheets and quickly filtered through them, picking out one with the most romantic title. She batted her eyelashes as he played, trying to subtly seduce him.

After he finished performing, Mickey enquired why Chanele had taken such an interest to him, seeing as she was considered by most to be a self-absorbed narcissist, definitely not someone who would care about others. She smiled, showing her stupidly perfect white teeth and revealed that she thought he was unbelievably talented and handsome, and that she would listen to him play forever.

She smiled at him again, watching his concerned expression with malicious intent.

"Emphasis on the handsome.", she winked.

Mickey pulled back, intimidated by her hastiness. How stupid of her to think he would fall for a manipulative snob like her? He deserves better than a stupid girl who's been with more guys than she could count on two hands, a woman that men keep around as a trophy and nothing more. Besides her looks, there was really nothing to her.

"Sorry, you're not my type. I prefer brains over beauty." He uttered, feeling disgusted. As he walked away, he regretted giving her his time of day in the first place.

"You know what, I didn't need you anyway." Chanele snapped, though he was too far to hear her.

"His loss." Chanele mumbled to herself

in attempt to soothe the sting of his rejection, begging that he wouldn't tell anyone. That would be so embarrassing. Why didn't he say yes? She didn't get it, Mickey looked like a million dollar man, so why was her heart broke? Chanele, too, was perfect, *beautiful*! Even if he didn't like her physique there were plenty of other good features about her. Had he not noticed a single one? She was even generous enough to actually *listen* to what he was saying - she didn't do that very often. How could he take that for granted? Then a horrible realisation dawned on her.

*What if I've gained weight?* She replayed herself walking up to him in her head, imagining how the weight on her arms jiggled, how her stomach formed rolls of lard when she bent over to pick up his music sheets. She had been skipping some meals recently, but maybe it wasn't enough. Maybe she needed to eat even less, even hit the gym. God, she'd had too many carbs, with almost no protein recently. Of course she was bloated, despite the caloric deficit she was in she was only consuming a few pastries. Mickey must like thin girls. Like Kate Moss? She reached for the Fibre One brownie in her pocket and put it in the bin. It wasn't that high-calorie, but every binge starts with a bite.

# Chapter 13

# The Last Supper

Mickey stood still, his mouth slack and

gaping open. Whilst Chanele's confession was hardly a surprise, practically nobody thought she would actually act on her deranged desire (Mickey included). He attempted to play a couple more notes but it was impossible. He couldn't get Chanele and her artificial smile out of his head.

It wasn't as if he wanted to date Chanele. She was just a Barbie doll as far as he was concerned. Plastic. *Fake*. Chanele had been played as much as his guitar and Mickey didn't want to be around someone like her.

As Mickey finished tuning the final string, he heard the Dinner Alarm go off - loud and piercing. Even though he had heard the lunch and breakfast bell a few hours prior, hearing another startled him even more.

The noise was almost blocked out by the sound of various instruments being dropped onto the ground. Mickey immediately did the same, propping up his guitar in the corner of the practice room. He opened the maple wood door and stepped into the occupied corridor.

It was positively swarming with frantic students of all ages, a subdued Chanele included. Mickey looked away quickly, his eyes swerving towards the rouge carpet.

Travelling briskly through the immense school, Mickey navigated his way round the propaganda-covered history lecture halls, and finally walked through the decorated canteen entrance. Everyone funnelled into the room, ravenous. So was he, despite the fact he had eaten only an hour ago.

Scrutinising the large hall, Mickey eventually discovered his seat, the words Mickey Griffiths plastered on the top of his chair. He pulled the teak wood chair out from under the long, momentously decorated table and sat down, his eyes wandering towards his peers. He noticed a very bored looking Connor sitting in between Simsie and Paige having a animated conversation about writing.

He also saw Chanele sitting painfully on her own, shifting her body to face anywhere but him. Mickey almost felt sorry for her, until he remembered all the people she had hurt, him included. It wasn't typical for him to reject someone without giving a heart-felt apology, but Chanele didn't deserve his pity. Still, he couldn't help giving her the occasional glance until he stood up, his plastic tray clenched a little too hard in his grip.

Chanele was neurotic. It didn't help that she kept on getting put-out glances from everyone she tried to talk to, or that she swore Mickey was staring at her every 5 seconds. It wasn't as if he had any reason to be mad, surely any guy would leap under a truck for the chance to be with her. Whatever, his loss. He was out of her league anyway.

It was time to get her dinner, which wasn't a necessarily good thing but at least it would occupy people long enough for her to sneak her food out. Usually dry fasting didn't really work on her, but this time was different. Even though she didn't see much of a result yet, she knew if she tried hard enough she could make this weight peel off. Hopefully her new body would make Mickey fall in love with her. That was the plan.

Chanele stood up, her heart lodged in her throat, and strode over to the counter. As she was analysing the food for the most solid option, she accidentally bumped into Simsie. Simsie flushed a little, smiling nervously at her.

"Sorry Chanele." She mumbled, wringing her hands together anxiously.

Chanele ignored Simsie's half-hearted apology and instead jolted past her, taking refuge at the front of the line. She smiled at the server, holding her tray out to him expectantly.

"Hi Will!" Chanele said, attempting to make her voice as bright and loud as possible.

"Hello Chanele. What will it be today?" Will asked, brandishing his ladle.

Chanele took a deep breath. "Hmm, I think I'll get the... veggie fingers, please. With chips and no ketchup." In reality, she knew exactly what to get. Anything dry would work well enough.

Will obligingly gave her a small helping of veggie fingers and chips, before shooing her away to deal with his next customer.

Chanele sat down again, noticing Diffshire a couple meters away from her, staring intently. That would make it harder, but not impossible. If it worked the first time, it would work again. She grabbed her fork and pretended to eat a mouthful of chips, instead dropping a few into her sweaty palm.

Once she found herself in a loop, it became much easier. With every 'bite' she

took, all the food somehow found its way
into her lap. Oops! It was a good thing
her pockets were only just large enough
to store most of the food, even the small
servings here were larger then what she
was used to, usually making sure her meal
wasn't bigger than her fist, taking small
bites, chewing well with sips of water in
between. Dr Diffshire walked away to have
a chat with Will, which was a good opportunity to grab her napkin and scoop up
the remains of her dinner.

She had done it. A surge of relief swept
over her, the ringing bell to commence the
end of dinner, was music to her ears. A
dinner lady peered at Chanele's empty plate
before shooing her away. *Gladly,* she thought,
standing up and waltzing out of the door
like the supermodel she dreamed of becom-

ing.

# Chapter 14

# Hidden Identity

'Welcome to the Art and Design Society' A red banner hung from two sides of the room. A table was stacked high with party food, cheese and pineapple sticks, pork pies, scotch eggs, you name it. Despite the full atmosphere, the area was scarce of people, and only Chanele and Connor were there, their aura filling a room for at least 30.

Chanele looked away from Connor, and walked to a fashion design display. She held the silk fabrics of a dress, and stroked them between her hands. It reminded her of when she was her aunt's bridesmaid, over 5 years ago. The soft music of the wedding reception, letting her sway freely. It was in a church, her family was always very religious. It was fun. But it was hard to remember. She tried to think about what happened, about how she felt, but it was all a blurry mess.

Now she was thinking about it, did it even happen?

Connor stared at a quaint water-coloured flower field, his eyes travelling across the page as he did so. While patiently observing, his gaze drifted and landed on Chanele, her hands travelling up a blue silk gown, in a world of her own.

"Chanele? Are you okay?" It was Connor. She snapped her head around and saw someone. It wasn't Connor. Well, it was, but he was different somehow. A long scar stretched across his face, and he was short.

"Connor?" Chanele looked at him, terrified.

"Yes?" His skin was paler then usual, and he was gently swaying from side to side. He looked more delicate, more vulnerable then usual. Chanele was scared, he looked ghostly, like he was about to pass out.

"Are you alright?" Chanel whispered. "You're all pale, and you have this scar on your cheek."

"What? No I don't." Connor nervously touched his face, before taking it off, relieved. "I'm fine. Are *you* feeling alright?"

Chanele looked over at the silk dress, and immediately remembered being a bridesmaid again. She remembered it all, the dinner, the dessert that spilled on her dress, being beaten for it afterwards. She had no idea why she didn't remember it before. Her head snapped back to Connor, and he was much taller, with no scar. He was normal. What was she thinking?

112

"I'm so sorry, Connor. I don't know what happened." He looked at her strangely and went back to looking at the paintings on the wall. Chanele stared down at her shoes, her new black slides and sighed. What was that about? Maybe it was another hallucination. She had been having lots recently. Yeah, it was probably just another one of them.

*But what if it wasn't…?*

# Chapter 15

# The Lollipop

NOTES:

Back to the control room, I noticed a strange figure pondering around the school that I've never seen before. Then I suddenly remembered Dr Diffshire presenting me a report of what the students actually look like when they don't eat enough. I regarded through the cameras a shorter student, with scars all over his face and brunette hair. As I recognised his identity, I could feel sweat beading down my face, watery marks appearing on the mouse as I urged to get a closer look.

I continued searching for what I could do. My heart managed to return to a normal pace as I figured a solution, breathing slowly and quietly. I looked at the coding screen and started typing rapidly, fingers teleporting to the keyboard. After around ten minutes, full of continuous struggle, I typed in the code.

```html
<html>

<head><title>

Code/Protocol test #1 title>

</head>

<body>

Intelligence test code = students

protocol

Dystopian fantasy configuration

Code complete... testing
```

```
testing</body>
```

```
</html>
```

I flicked to another camera, I saw Will
in the kitchen. He had spotted Chanele
stuffing food in her pockets at lunch. But
what should he have done? Told the teachers? That might have gotten her in trouble. What if he had got some nicer food
for her to eat? That might have worked.

Scrambling around the kitchen, Will was
searching for food for Chanele. It would
have to be nice otherwise she wouldn't eat
it. What would a student eat as a snack?
Every cupboard was opened and empty,
but he still had no luck. Until he saw a
glistening package at the very back of one

of his many shelves. Most people would've needed a stool but fortunately, Will was tall enough to reach it. He leaned into the cupboard and grasped the first thing he touched. What lay in his hand was a singular, dark red, cherry lollipop. Perfect.

As soon as Will had found his snack for Chanele, he hurried out of the kitchen to search for her. Luckily for him, she was just down the hall. He strolled over to her anxiously. Without making a fuss he pulled her aside and asked to speak to her.

"Erm hi, " Will spoke nervously. "Not sure if you remember me or not but I serve food in the canteen, ".

"Hi... yeah I do remember you." Chanele replied "Why are you speaking to me?"

"Err, I saw you weren't eating at lunch, " Will was sweating. "I'm not sure if the food was nice enough or not so I brought you a lollipop."

"Oh. Well, thanks, I guess." Chanele accepted the lollipop and walked away.

Before Chanele left his sight, Will stopped her. He grabbed her shoulder and told her "Make sure you eat it, I'm worried."

"Don't. Touch. Me." Chanele stormed off. Making her way down the hallway, She stared at the lollipop, thinking about whether to eat it or not. *Ninety calories,* a voice warned. She was meant to be fasting today. Was that too much? She couldn't break her fast for a stupidly sugary confection. But.. it was only a lollipop.

Chanele's stomach rumbled at the thought of food. She gave in, like a ravenous animal tearing apart their prey. She slowly peeled off the pink wrapper and held it in her hand. She stared at it, hesitantly. She lifted her hand that held the lollipop tightly up to her mouth and licked it. Saliva built up in her mouth, forcing her to have another taste. The artificial cherry flavours melted against her tongue, soothing her taste buds. In that moment, shame conquered all of her other emotions, causing her hunger to simmer in the pit of her stomach instead of coursing through her.

\* \* \*

Control room. The robotic, female voice could be heard, the same one that was always played when something went wrong. Simple error. Easy fix.

"Just need a few more lines of coding here, double check for any syntax errors." I anticipated. After a few minutes that felt like seconds, a sudden grin stretched my muscles in my jaw as a sign of pride. Everything was under control.

# Chapter 16

# Truth Revealed

Chanele stood there and stirred her coffee with a spoon and a worried face on. Paige noticed and became concerned - she knew something was wrong, but she didn't know what, so she questioned the blonde.

"You've been stirring that coffee for 5 minutes, usually you down it in 5 seconds! What's wrong with you? You've been acting so *different* lately." Paige took a large gulp of her hot chocolate and looked deeply into Chanele's harsh, brown eyes, exuding a cold blanket around the two of them.

Chanele lifted her head and her face drooped even more as she muttered, "I don't know." But Paige could tell she was hiding something.

Paige added with a low tone "You know you can trust me Chanele, we've known each other since highschool!" Paige was getting fed up, whatever Chanele was hiding, she was being pathetic about it. But could she really? For as comfortable of a companion as Paige had become, she'd remained as utterly unreadable as ever. Every now and then, words appeared on the page, forming coherent sentences, but Chanele struggled to follow the plot. If she didn't say something, however, Paige would figure it out on her own. She was smart - that's why Chanele had let her in her social circle - but *too* smart for her liking. What if she figured out she hadn't been eating, mistook it for an eating disorder, and tried to intervene? That wouldn't do.

Chanele took a deep breath, her head pounding. "I've been hallucinating lately. I think it's because I'm not eating. I'm not starving myself like an anorexic or whatever, I just think there's something in the food. I've been seeing this weird place, like a hospital, or a mental asylum. The longer I go without eating, the more often I see it."

Paige stared at her in wonder and misbelief. She had also heard some stories, but she kept quiet, edging Chanele to keep talking.

"It's not just the world around me, it's people too. Like Connor, when we were signing up for societies, he looked all different, with a scar on his cheek. It was deep. Really deep, and it didn't look like it had been treated properly. It was discoloured, almost looked like a rainbow spread across his face. Shades of blue, purple and brown surrounded the area of the laceration. I don't think it was self-inflicted, he doesn't seem like the kind of guy who'd do that. It was like someone had done it to him. On purpose?"

Paige nodded and let Chanele know that she would always be there for her. Her hand reached out to hold Chanele's, and they both smiled at each other, like a peace treaty in a world of warfare.

Sat on the table behind them, Mickey was watching them, listening into their conversation. *What a weirdo!* He thought. Maybe she was insane, or had schizophrenia. He wouldn't put it against her, she saw things that weren't real all the time. Like people enjoying her company. She's sooooo fake.

Mickey wandered around the cafeteria, coming towards a table full of people. "You know Chanele? She's got schizophrenia, seeing weird things. I wouldn't talk to her if I were you. It may be *contagious.* You don't wanna end up an object like her."

The students gasped, muttering incoherent words under their breath. Mickey smiled to himself, proud of what he had done. Happy at the situation he had created. Chanele deserved it, he thought. In fact, she deserved a LOT worse. This was a child's punishment for everything she had done.

As the words spread, people started constructing opinions. Mostly negative. Most people start to call Chanele an outcast, a traitor in society.

Roughly an hour later, everyone was talking and whispering about Chanele, negatively. They were calling her crazy; mad. A few people even said she was doing it for attention - Chanele *always* wants attention. Though, she only liked being in the spotlight when she was admired, not abhorred. The rumour had spread like wildfire smoke gliding through everyone's lips. Soon, the whole university was aware of the 'weird' first year who starved herself and hallucinated.

People were calling her a monster, saying she belonged in a mental hospital. And if you disliked Chanele before, you *definitely* hated her now. She was the university's newest freak and there was no stopping that now.

# Chapter 17

# Chasing Craig

The landscape appeared to be barren,

lifeless, with nothing prospering among the sea of crimson and vermilion leaves. The branches of each tree hung limply like the limbs of a rotten corpse, each bush shrivelled and deformed, forming peculiar shapes and throwing perplexing shadows onto the grounds.

However, among it all, the tall and slim, blonde haired silhouette of Miss Lancaster briskly strolled through the troupes of leaves, spewing them everywhere. She was on a mission. A mission to find Craig. She came to a stop at the corner of one of the universities aged stone walls, eagerly edging forward. She had spotted Craig trimming some of the hedges which still had a shred of life left within them.

Cautiously, she pulled herself forward, sliding closer and closer towards him. But before she could come any closer than two meters of Craig, Alan and Smudge strode over to him. A conversation began, which Miss Lancaster could only catch snippets of from such a great distance.

But she wasn't interested in what they were talking about. She retreated, disheartened. Her attempt to talk to Craig had turned out dreadfully.

She dragged her feet through the early autumn foliage, mind empty, listening to the voice of the wind's lively whisper amongst the branches of the trees. Instantaneously, the shrill sound of a dog's bark broke through the heavy silence clouding her mind. She turned around, quickly and cautiously, her palms sweating, her pupils dilating, her body shaking. But her feelings of fear were wasted, for it was only the small sausage dog, Doug, that bounded around her, jumping up and down ecstatically.

Nonetheless, Miss Lancaster was still startled from hearing the intrusive barking, and did not wish to get soil over her clothes (as she had noticed that the dog was dressed in layers of mud and amber coloured leaves). Gingerly, she creeped backwards, turned, and broke into a sprint, her heavy footsteps crushing the leaves, leaving behind what sounded like the crinkling of a fire.

Puzzled, yet unflustered, Doug clumsily picked up a pair of small, green gardening scissors with his mouth and bounced happily back to where he had came from, with a spring in his step. He was a very energetic dog. The perfect companion for a man like Craig. Within a few moments, he had arrived before Craig, to whom he gave the scissors to.

"You're a very good dog, " he remarked, and gave Doug a treat. Doug licked his lips swiftly. Craig watched as the tiny dachshund spun around, merrily wagging his tail. Smudge, who lay on his back and was motionless, growled in envy.

# Chapter 18

# Glimpse Into Reality

A creak broke out through the winding halls. The old lift opened, and out of it emerged Paige. She saw Connor, lent against a tall wall with patterned wallpaper and a small lamp above his head, the light circling him like a halo. He was doodling in his shabby notebook (that somehow was still not full), on his own, and she rushed over to him.

"Where have you been? I've been looking for you everywhere!" sighed Paige, catching her breath.

"I've been here the whole time, I'm going to my dorm." Connor's deep voice replied.

"I don't care about that, have you heard about Chanele hallucinating!" Paige's voice sounded eager, yet a hint of confusion could be heard in her words.

"Yeah, at the club yesterday, she started saying my face looked different."

"She told me that she's been seeing some weird place like a hospital or a mental asylum."

"She started talking about scars on my face that aren't even there."

"You haven't got any scars on your face, I think she's hallucinating again." Paige stared at his face, checking for any scarring.

"She's probably just trying to find another way to get attention from everyone, but I didn't think she was this desperate."

Paige mumbled, "What if she's right?"

"What was that?" Connor turned around so he was facing her.

"Nothing, I'm just thinking about what

if she's right about the hallucinations."

"What, so we're in some weird dream which we all share, no that's impossible!" Connor laughed under his breath at the suggestion.

"Yeah, she's probably wrong." Paige shrugged.

Connor thought about it for a moment. "Have you noticed how she hasn't been eating lately?"

"Yeah, why?"

"She's stopped eating then she starts hallucinating, don't you think that it could just be the food." Connor suggested, stroking his chin thoughtfully.

"She told me that the more she doesn't eat the more often she hallucinates and sees this hospital or mental asylum, but it's only been a few days, it takes longer to start hallucinating than just a few days." Paige reminded him.

"It might not be right but I think that's the reason why and she's going crazy because of it!"

"Yeah, maybe. I'm still not convinced though."

The corridors were covered in paintings, gold panels crowding the walls like an antidote concealing a virus, the walls engulfed in black marble. Countless students passed by, all of them silent, bleeding into the background like a dream or a character embedded into a game.

Paige leaned back against the wall as Connor explained, "I heard about Mickey spreading rumours about Chanele."

"What did he say?"

"He's been talking about Chanele going

crazy and having hallucinations."

"Who do you believe?"

"I believe Mickey, what about you.?" Connor replied instantly.

Paige pondered for a moment "I think that Mickey is right and I understand why they would believe Mickey, but there's no need to be so horrible to Chanel and tease her about it."

"If you believe Mickey then prove to me that he's right." Paige finally said.

Connor rolled his eyes. "For example, we went to the club last night, we were both there, if this was fake and we were dreaming, why wouldn't we both have the same dream?"

"That's only one night though, how else is this real?" Paige replied, though she knew he had a very good point.

"At breakfast, lunch, and dinner we were all there eating, drinking and talking to each other, how could all of that be fake.? Connor added.

"Fine! I believe you but I still think that she could have been right. What are we going to do about Chanel, we can't just let her be teased by everyone." Paige looked miserable.

"Yes we can, she's a narcissistic, self-absorbed parasite."

"That doesn't matter, she's still my friend so I need to do something about it."

"Alright then but your doing it on your own, I'm not helping her spread her delusion to others." Connor reminded Paige as she stormed away.

As she made her way through campus, Paige saw the hallway flicker between a corridor of the university and somewhere else, like white void. The air felt heavy and damp, sticking in her throat. It was too bright, the walls painted a sickly shade of white and the potted plant gone. The strange thing was that the layout stayed the exact same the entire time, almost as if she was in the same place in different times. Swivelling her head around desperately, she noticed a figure her age at the other end of the corridor. Connor.

"Connor!" She shouted, running towards the shadowy figure.

Connor turned and looked for Paige, only to see a short, dark haired girl who definitely wasn't his friend.

"Paige?" yelled Connor, glancing around trying to find Paige.

"Connor?" The strange girl answered,

her large doe eyes watering.

"Who are you?" replied Connor whilst searching for the black marble walls shrouding the corridors.

"Paige!" The girl replied incredulously.

"You're not Paige."

"Yes I am, where's Connor?" She blinked in shock, taking in this strange looking man.

"I'm Connor!"

"No you're not, you have scars all over your body, your short and you have a beard." Paige smiled nervously, praying this was all a big misunderstanding.

"Like Chanele told me at the club…" Connor said, his smile dropping.

"What if she was right?" Paige looked down at her arms, checking to see if she looked different too.

"That's impossible, this isn't fake, it can't be."

"Yes it can, Chanele was right."

"What about the other people here, are they real?"

"I think they are, we can't find out right now we'll have to wait and ask Chanele about how we stop seeing this delusion and see the real world."

"Fine, I'll wait!" Connor snapped, infuriated. He stormed to his dorm, Paige following sheepishly behind.

# Chapter 19

# Diffshire's Dilemma

NOTES:

I was sitting in my chair, typing away at a quite rapid speed. As my fingers teleported between keys, typing away pieces of coding, I could hear loud thudding coming from the hallway behind me, sounding like a drum beat every interval of a second. I like keeping notes of things, it makes me remember key information better and also key events that need addressing. Suddenly, the door swung wide open creating a slight creak sound as it rotated around the door hinges. I turned around rapidly to see what the commotion was about and it was Dr Diffshire. "Oh great, what have I done wrong now?" I thought to myself, "I'm totally fired or something bad, aren't I?"

Surprisingly enough, she didn't arrive at my room to complain about me. Instead she was complaining about the students. She proclaimed that people weren't eating and they started to have hallucinations about reality. She told me everything, tears building up like a tidal wave ready to hit the sea bank, her speech becoming more serious but at the same time annoyed as she continued. She kept saying how students start to see the actual picture, a glitch in the camera only they can start to see.

She exclaimed how she needs to get rid of them as soon as possible. I thought about it at first and said "Why don't we hold an intelligence test and each student has their own test for them which is actually their real world weakness. I can code and make the test for you, all you need to do is somehow get them into the test." After hearing that, she paused for a few seconds and exclaimed, "Sure, great idea. But how long do you think you'll need to build and code it? I don't want these students to get worse and overthrow us in power." After that I said, " I see, give me 12 hours and quite a lot of resources and a few private locations. I'm going to need them."

"I understand." Dr Diffshire said. "Although, how are you thinking on getting them in?". After a hot minute, I replied.

"Maybe you could host a quick speech on the curriculum or stimulus and then after keep behind the people who are hallucinating? Either way it'll have to be something to do with the university." I turned

around to get back on with the stupid coding.

"OK then. I shall leave you to get on
with whatever you are doing and I will
come back here to give an update on the
situation." Dr Diffshire blurted.

She spun on her heels like she was in a
ballet routine and left with a satisfied expression on her face, noticing a grin start
to emerge from her cheek muscles. I got to
work immediately, taking her orders into
careful consideration attempting not to mess
up anything or else that would probably
get me fired.

# Chapter 20

# Tears of the Teased

Chanele tiptoed quietly up the stairs, trying to reach her bedroom before anyone else. After the incident with Mickey, and everyone spreading rumours about her, she knew that she would be a target for bullies.

All she had to do was to make it to her room in time. The marble walls around her, the ones that usually echoed so much noise, remained silent. She was safe, there was nobody around. Everyone was most likely sheltered away in the student union, drinking and socialising, playing stupid games.

As she reached the final staircase, she glanced into the tall mirror beside her, her sharp features reflecting in the pearly glass. She stared at her silky blonde hair, before removing the hair tie. It had to look perfect, she thought. She tossed it behind her and re-did her ponytail, tightening it so much that it stretched and ripped her scalp.

Whilst tightening her ponytail, she heard the familiar patter of footsteps, and immediately ran off, trying to escape the voices she heard, echoing closer. Her designer flat shoe snapped off her foot and started rolling down the staircase, landing squarely in front of Mickey.

Chanele hesitated, before running to get her shoe. It was very expensive, and she didn't want it to break. The group of students in front of her started giggling, insults sliding in between their sequenced laughs. "Really? For a shoe?" Someone asked.

"No wonder Mickey rejected you!" Simsie announced, gasps emerging in the crowd. Chanele's eyes started to water. Why were they doing this? What did she do to hurt them?

She looked into the crowd, noticing Paige and Connor standing there, motionless. Staring into Paige's eyes, Chanele knew that she was going to stick up for her. She believed her, didn't she? She told Paige everything in student union, all about the visions, and the nightmares!

Paige remained silent, and so did Connor beside her. They just watched and stared as Mickey berated her, ignoring the painful tears streaming from Chanele's eyes.

Mickey walked up to Chanele, a harsh expression on his face. He called her crazy, watching as her face switched from sadness to pure hysteria.

"I'm not crazy here, all of you are. Your a bunch of delusional, mind-controlled freaks that don't see the real issue!" She shouted, but even she started to believe it too. Seeing all these images, having all these terrifying dreams, maybe she *was* insane after all. Chanele walked away, reaching in her pocket. There was a loose gummy bear, collecting dust in the depths of her jacket. She picked it up, thinking about eating it. Food always made everyone else feel better, maybe it would make her feel better too?

She put it to her lips, before snatching it away. No. If she wanted love, if she wanted to be a Victoria's Secret Angel, she needed to work for it. She dropped the gummy bear on the floor, no food for the hardworking. The fact that she even considered it in the first place was repulsive. Was she really just about to ruin her progress for a bite? All the food she craved would still be there when she reached her goal weight. Her thinspiration would most definitely *not* act like this.

Once in her enclosed bedroom, Chanele sunk into the linen sheets, creating damp patches with her tears. Her life was officially ruined. Everybody hated her. Even the people she told everything to, the people who she trusted, had left her in the depressing, slowly caving hole of her life. God, she was so pathetic right now, maybe it would be better if she wasn't here at all. She lingered on the thought longer than she'd like to admit, but decided against it. What if in her next life she was a morbidly obese slob? Her current situation was a *way* better alternative. Plus, she didn't have the best karmic lineage, meaning she'd probably be born as the one thing she's desperately trying to avoid.

She stared at her mascara-stained pillows. At least she was pretty when she cried. What wasn't pretty, however, was the way everyone was ridiculing her despite the fact that most people didn't so much as speak to her. They judged her like a picture book, by the colours like they forgot to read. She was more than her flawless frame, she had other qualities, right? She was charming, funny, social. Why couldn't they see that? Everyone was so caught up in seeing her negatives - if she even had any - that they forgot to think of her as a person. She knows she messed up, but she's just a young girl in the world.

Can't she do the best they can?

# Chapter 21

# Karma

Mickey couldn't believe how deeply Chanele went to get attention; he thought she was insane. Full of himself, he bounded over to Simsie and said "Have you heard what Chanele has been saying? She's gone mad! She said she could see some other world!"

Simsie repeated "She can see another world?"

While laughing Mickey replied "Yeah she's so crazy!"

Simsie laughed with him. They talked for a little more about what was happening. They both agreed that the hallucinations people were having were really odd. Simsie decided not to tell him that weird things were happening to her too. Afterwards, Mickey told Simsie to spread the word around, that he wanted everyone to know what was wrong with her.

When he finished telling Simsie about Chanele, the rumours started spreading like a virus, mutating until the rumour came back to him and it sounded like a whole different story. He went back to his dorm after dinner. When he started to change, his mind went cloudy and his vision started to go blurry, his eyes started to flicker and his skin went pale. He felt like he was going to pass out.

'Maybe I just need some sleep...'

As soon as he sat down on his bed, Mickey started to feel dizzy. He felt like he wanted to throw up. His body felt weak. Then he started to see this dreadful room with grey wallpaper pealing off the walls and creaky floorboards that felt weak under his feet, he was mortified, he didn't know what was happening as he never had any of those dreams or hallucinations before.

He didn't like it, he wanted to get out of there but the hallucinations just wouldn't stop. He was scared and he started panicking.

His dorm started turning into dark and gloomy hospital room with peeling walls and cold floors, his guitar turned into a wheelchair, his bed turned into a hospital bed with filthy sheets. He looked down at what he was wearing and he saw a hospital gown, stained with crusty patches of blood.

He hated everything about this, he just wanted to go back to his normal dorm in his normal clothes. He was terrified. He shouted at the top of his voice "OH MY GOD WHAT IS HAPPENING!"

164

Nobody was there to hear his cries for help. He knelt down, tears streaming from his eyes.

Mickey started to realise that Chanele was right and he felt kind of bad about all the things he was saying about her to everyone. He felt he should apologise and stop the rumour, tell everyone that this weird other world was real and not just a way to get attention.

Mickey had totally forgot about the strange world he was in and was worrying to much about Chanele. As the world started coming into focus, he realised that he was still there but slowly fading. He could start to see his dorm room coming back again.

As the room fully materialised, he let out a sigh of relief and started to feel normal again. He wasn't dizzy or weak anymore. He just felt like his normal self.

Whilst falling asleep, he remembered poor Chanele. He knew that he needed to make things right tomorrow, no matter what it took.

# Chapter 22

# Last Breakfast

The sun was suprisingly late to rise this

morning. Usually, the sun would have woken Chanele and Simsie up at around 5 am, yet that morning the light that shone on Chanele and Simsie's pillows was delayed by almost 3 hours.

Simsie was up after Chanele; who had already left for breakfast. That wasn't a good sign (usually they got up at around the same time). Now that it was the next day, Simsie really started to regret the things she had said to Chanele. Although she was full of herself, she was still a girl, just like her. Maybe Simsie was just jealous that a girl her age could look like a supermodel *and* be surrounded by people. Simsie was already aware she was too soft, too boyish to be pretty; and too shy to talk to anyone other than herself.

When she looked at her little tin alarm

clock, the time read 7:50. More than enough time to get a shower and put on some actual clothes.

After getting ready and presentable, Simsie walked down the long staircase and excited the dormitories. She stretched across the long, freshly-trimmed grass, ready and excited for breakfast. Her appetite was usually small enough to sustain a day without eating: but that caused dizziness and terrible dreams. Plus, if she wanted to continue playing tennis, she needed to nourish her body. Sport was the only thing she was good at, people actually seemed interested in what she had to say when she was up on the court.

The corridors weren't as busy today, possibly because everyone had arrived early; the alarm hadn't even gone off yet. Simsie found her friends pretty easily, standing next to Paige like always. One thing that felt different today was Mickey and Chanele sharing silent stares, and drowning in a sea of silence for a minute until they decided to speak up.

"Guys, we need to talk." That made everyone's head turn. He cleared his throat nervously. "Me and Chanele have been talking."

That was startling. As far as everyone in the corridors was concerned, Mickey and Chanele were worst enemies. The fact that they had been conversing with one and another sounded like a recipe for disaster.

Chanele gave him a grateful look, before adding, "I know some of you guys have been talking about me. About how

I'm crazy and stuff. Well I'm *not.*" Everyone blinked. Simise didn't really believe Chanele's protest, everyone knew she wasn't quite sane and why.

Mickey looked pale and tired. "It's true. I know it's true."

"Why?" Paige asked, her brow furrowing in confusion.

"It's happening to me too."

As soon as he announced this new information, the entire group collapsed into a mixture of chaos and dubiety. Mickey was being bombarded with millions of questions all related to his most recent statement, and for once Chanele was getting looks of sympathy, not hatred. After all of the friends compared their symptoms of the past day or two, they all realised they shared kindred experiences.

Chanele beamed, clearly basking in her newfound attention. "So, what we think right now is that maybe this isn't the real world. That we're somehow trapped in a fictional reality and we need to escape."

For a moment, everyone was silent, slowly taking in this new information.

After a couple minutes, Connor spoke up. "How do we get out? And how do you know?"

Chanele looked up at him, dark eyes vague and expressionless. "It's the food. We think, well we know, that they're drugging the food."

Paige looked skeptical, and Simsie cleared her throat, concerened. "So, do we just not eat? Won't we be hungry?"

Chanele shrugged."Maybe, i guess?"

Everbody at the turned to look at eachother, eyes blazing with intent.

Concurrently, everyone spoke, only audible to those who listened attentivley.

"It's a plan."

Miss Lancaster knew she shouldn't of been listening; every bone in her body said to turn around and forget what she had just heard. Except now that she had ascertained the reason for Chanele's hallucinations, she couldn't get it out of her head. No matter how much Miss Lancaster wanted to keep their conversation a secret; she knew deep down it wasn't ethical.

So after a few minutes of contemplation, she finally decided to tell Will. It was only because she noticed Paige turn around to whisper to a ginger girl walking past, who consequently stopped eating her waffle. The news was spreading like wildfire and someone needed to put it out.

"Will?" She asked, slipping around the corner to speak with him.

Will looked pleasantly suprised. "What's up?" He replied.

"All the kids, they've started protesting about the food. They think it's being drugged." She responded wearily, wringing her pale hands.

Will looked distraught. "Wh..what?"

"I'm going to call Dr Diffshire." She responded stoutly, looking on into the empty hall, preparing for the worst.

# Chapter 23

# Let the Games Begin

Dr Diffshire walked into the cafeteria and heard screaming and shouting. To her right, she caught a glimpse of teachers and students running in to see what the racket was about. As they sprinted past her, Dr Diffshire had a peeked through the door and saw that the students were chanting "FIX OUR FOOD, FIX OUR FOOD." Dr Diffshire started to realise that they were getting to aware and they might have been able to escape the simulation. She knew what she had to do.

Dr Diffshire then walked through the main hall and climbed the steep staircase. She saw a few students giggling on their way to their next lesson. In the corner of her eye she saw another one of the teachers presenting their lecture in their classrooms. She walked through the big corridors that proudly displayed students' work and posters stuck to the walls. She opened the white door to the IT room and slowly the colours bleed away from the university and the dark gloomy colours start to appear. When she stepped through the door she saw John sat on his chair typing on his computer. She sped over to him and shouts "JOHN, JOHN LISTEN TO THIS!"

John replies with "What do you want now?"

Dr Diffshire says with a shaky voice "The pills aren't working, they are wearing off, this cant happen! What do we do now?"

John says "It's time to get it ready!"

His fingers were a blur - lines of code flooded the screen as John entered the final keystrokes. He shouted Dr Diffshire over and said "Done."

Dr Diffsire replied with "We did it!"

John said "*I* did it. The test is ready - now we just have to get them to take it."

"No one will ever be willing to take the test - they have become to aware over everything. They know we put the pill in the food! There is no absolute way they would take a test if we told them to, they would go mad." Dr Diffshire began.

"That's why I have another plan." John replied.

Dr Diffshire said "Did you know they have been having protests against us and no one will eat there food?"

John replied snarkily. "Yeah, don't you think I know?"

"So what's the plan then?" Dr Diffshire

questioned.

John mulled it over. "Nitrous oxide."

Dr Diffshire looked quizzically at him. "What's Nitrous oxide again?"

"A gas -we can pump it through the vents."

Dr Diffshire replied with a smirk "Good plan, John."

John replied cockily "I know."

Dr Diffshire questioned "So what's next then?"

John answered while rolling his eyes "You have to go and activate the gas to knock them out, *obviously.*"

"Oh, okay, then I best be off." she replied hastily.

"Yeah, go then"

Dr Diffshire asks "WAIT! Before I go, what do you want me to do while you do the coding?"

"All you need to do is check if everything is going to plan and then get out of there quick or you will get gassed"

"Okay"

Dr Diffshire walked through the control room and and saw the white door that lead back to the university She went for the handle, opened the door and all the vibrant colours started to illuminate the atmosphere around her. After she came through the door she started walking through the big corridor again and to her left she saw the same teacher, teaching her lesson still and she saw a few more students passing by. It was like she had never left the university. She strutted her way over to the cafeteria and started to make sure everything was working and the plan was going to work out just right. Diffshire went round to all the vents to check if everything was working and was ready in motion. She gave a thumbs up to John in the security camera to let his know everything was ready and the student were ready to be gassed at breakfast.

9:00. An ear-piercing alarm went off and a groups of students came piling in for breakfast. Dr Diffshire snuck out of the large hall to make sure all the teachers and students where in the cafeteria. John secretly watched through the security cameras and saw that everyone was in the cafeteria and he knew.. It was time.

John started to write the code in, his plan was going perfectly. As his finger tapped on the keys he got to the final part. Then he was ready, he took one more look at the security to make sure Dr Diffshire wasn't in there, he pressed the last key. Gas slowly started evacuating the vents and into the cafeteria air. Connor anxiously turns to Mickey and says "I'm starting to feel kind of light-headed"

"I'm starting to feel a bit dizzy too" Mickey replied while sluring his words. Mickey and Connor looked around and saw that people started to slowly fall to the ground one by one.

In the security cameras John knew his plan was working perfectly and everything was going just right. He kept an eye on the security cameras and made sure all the teachers and students passed out. He specifically kept an extra eye on the people that he had doubts on in the simulation. Nothing got in the way of his plan and he knew everything was going to be just fine..

# Chapter 24

# The Chaos Has Come

The alarm sounded, a loud blaring echoed through the students' heads. A constant reminder that it was time to eat once again. But were they going to eat this time? No. People flooded into the cafeteria, shouting and protesting against the fact that they were being forced to eat meals that were laced with some sort of pretending drug.

The teachers tried their hardest to prevent the rebellion before they had to go to their more drastic measures. It was all in haste, however, as before they knew it the worst scenario had already become reality. The rebellion had started, stronger than anyone could have ever predicted.

A group of people jumped onto the stretched oak tables that lined the large room. Although, however large the room could be it still couldn't of stopped the strange feeling that the four tall walls were keeping in the secrets of Dr Diffshire and her minions.

Back to the CCTV room, I sat at my desk typing in some last minute protocols for the intelligence test. Suddenly, I heard the phone to my left vibrate rapidly. I picked it up and put it to my ear. The voice on the other side was Dr Diffshire. Her tone is in a quite serious mode. She told me that the students were getting out of control, sort of protesting against the canteen staff. The chance of us surviving a protest of like one hundred students was next to nothing. Dr Diffshire told me to push a red button ONLY if things got out of control.

About 10 minutes passed, and the yelling

had become almost unbearable. I thought then would be the right time to use it. I pressed it and looked at the CCTV at the canteen. Some sort of gas started seeping out of the ventilation system. I started to type more code with a few errors and a voice saying "configuration complete, error detected, etc".

Gas started spewing out of the air vents. Students began to panic, jumping on top of table. Everyone was looking at one another seeing how to react. It began to rise higher and higher. The students began inhaling in the yellow fumes and of course they unexpectedly started feeling drowsy and light headed. Their heads were spinning as if their brains were in a tornado. I almost felt sorry for them, until i remembered the consequences of what would have happened if we didn't begin the test.

The tables stood in a formation and heads started dropping on the tables, fast asleep. Some passed out standing up and some just passed out on the floor; looking like a kid who had a bit too much of an energetic day. The students laid lifeless. Their faces decorated with a blank expression. The room was silent as the hissing of gas came to a quick stop. The doors creaked open as guards walked through picking up bodies and dragged them out of the hall. One by one, the bodies emptied out of the cafeteria leaving the room a desolate wasteland.

The test was ready. Every student, from the young to the old, short to the tall had been transported into their own rooms.

*where are they? Where are they?* The

test has begun...  The choice is theirs now..

# Chapter 25

# Level One:
# Training

TEST SUBJECT 1 AND 2 - Craig and Alan.

Everything was black, until the glamorous rays of the Sun interrupted their slumber. Alan and Craig awoke. They were lying down; beneath them was a soft, luscious mattress of grass. They were in an empty field. A deep, gravely voice echoed through the cold air. It said, "The key to your freedom is through a man's best friend, human or not. Freedom can be earned through the circumstances which you are close to. The choice is yours. Let the game begin!" The speaker ruffled like the sound of a static coming from a TV.

"Alan, did you hear that?" Craig whispered.

"Yes... yes I did." Alan answered.

Two dogs came running towards them, one big and one small. The small one was a light brown and the big one was a sandy-brown, almost white.

"Smudge and Doug?!" they both yelled in sync.

Craig and Alan both stood up and ran through the long, lush grass to the dogs. Smudge and Doug both jumped up with excitement; Craig and Alan caught them which caused Alan to tumble over. "Are you okay?" Craig asked in a worrying tone.

"Yeah, I'm fine. It's not like I've just been attacked by my MASSIVE dog!" Alan replied sarcastically. Laughter was shared between the two of them. Craig held out his hand; Alan took it and got back on his feet. After some time had past, Alan and Craig came to realise that they didn't actually know where they were.

"Craig, what did that voice say before?" Alan asked.

"Oh erm it said something about like freedom is the role of a man's best friend."

"Human or not... right?"

"Yeah I think so."

"But what does that mean?"

There was a long, silent pause.

"Oh my god, its about the dogs!" exclaimed Craig

"YES! What do we have to do with them? Play with them? Train them?"

"That's it, we have to train them!"

"What with though? We're in an empty field. There's nothing here."

"Then let's find something."

Standing up, they both scanned the grass, looking for clues. Alan squinted his eyes when he saw a patch of grass that was much lighter than the rest.

"Craig look at that over there! It doesn't look right."

"It looks like it could be a mat."

"No Craig, but it looks important. Come on, let's go."

Alan began to jog. Craig and the dogs followed. The terrain was different all throughout. Lumps and bumps along with in few dips on the ground didn't help with their journey. The out of breath men and the panting dogs made it there at last. They were met with a cardboard box. Craig and Alan stood, towering over the muddy-coloured box, waiting for it to open itself.

"Well open it then..." Craig suggested.

Alan edged towards the box and opened it hesitantly, his two hands trembling. Inside were dog treats, water bottles, bowls, leads and dog toys. Doug barked with excitement. Smudge was still panting and had started to drool over the dog treats.

Relief spread through each of their bodies when they saw what was inside the box.

"So I'm guessing we have to use the resources to train the dogs." uttered Craig.

"I guess so." answered Alan.

Craig peered into the box to see only one dog toy. He knew this was done purposely, but why? "Why would they put only one dog toy in here? Craig blurted. They must know that we both have a dog."

"It's clearly to make us work together." Alan replied.

Craig and Alan were both very independent people. They grew up without any family and taught themselves how to do everything on their own. They were both good friends but they both knew that they were going to struggle with the task. Alan and Craig seemed very resentful about the whole situation, yet they knew they had to persevere.

Smudge spotted the dog toy that Doug was playing with and raced after it. Whilst laughing, Alan shouted "Hey! Give that back!"

The dogs proceeded to play. A big stretch was preformed by Alan, signalling to Craig that he was about to stand up. The patch of tall, standing grass that they were both sat upon was now flattened. Dead.

"Doug! Smudge!" Craig shouted. The two groundskeepers began to run. Alan was limping due to his fall. They eventually caught up with the dogs (who had tired themselves out within a minute of playing and sprinting).

"I guess we have to train them now then, " Alan sighed.

"Sit!" Craig demanded. Doug obeyed him so he was rewarded with a treat. Alan tried to copy and do the same but was met with failure. Smudge had decided to roll over one hundred and eighty degrees and stop once his fluffy, warm back met the cold, hard grass. Frustrated, Alan turned around and said " Craig?"

"Yes, " he replied.

"Can you teach how to do that, please?"

"Yeah, sure!"

Over the hour, Craig and Alan helped one another train their dogs. They were desperately in need of some extra toys; as both the dogs became bored easily. Craig managed to keep them both occupied by running across the field on multiple occasions, subsequently getting overbalanced by Smudge's girthy frame. Fortunately, it was only about an hour before both Doug and Smudge could follow numerous simple tasks without fail.

Alan and Craig pondered about why they were still there and why they were sent there in the first place.

"I wonder what happens now" Alan said, breaking the silence.

"I'm not sure, I guess we just wait." Craig guessed.

A loud, manly voice boomed across the field. "Well done! You have completed your task and succeeded in over coming your weaknesses. A golden gate will appear on the other side of the field, through

that is your freedom." The ground shook
as the majestic gate formed from afar. The
bright golden colour of the gate was blinding yet beautiful, every single inch of it was
elaborately detailed, it looked like something out of a dream. Alan and Craig's
eyes widened at their view. They froze.
Every single bone in each of their bodies
became stiff.

"What has just happened?" whispered
Craig

"I don't know." Alan answered wor-
riedly

"Come on!" Craig jumped up and began to head to the glorious gate. Alan and
the dogs followed behind. First it began as
a walk, then it turned into a jog and then it
was a run. Hope filled their minds. Hope
of a way out. All four of them halted once

they approached their golden ticket home. They stood there in a daze, their jaws were dropped and their legs unsteady. This was it.

"Let's go!" Alan exclaimed.

"3!"

"2!"

"1!"

Craig, Alan, Doug and Smudge rushed towards their escape.

# Chapter 26

# Level Two: Height and Insecurities

TEST SUBJECT 3 - Mickey.

I opened my eyes slowly, my head was aching. *what had happened?* I looked around the room. It was small with cracked grey walls and it smelt of blood and rust. I felt myself beginning to panic, when suddenly, a deeper, male voice started to reverberate around the room in a speaker.

He exclaimed, "Let it begin. This appraisal is brought to this room for something that isn't a personal spite or appearance, but a test of logic and perspective. Make the choice, it's up to you."

I looked around, all I saw were a few weak boxes. They looked like they would collapse to even a slight breeze, and a large red button. I walked over to the wall which the button was placed. I jumped up frantically trying to press down onto the shiny red surface. *'Why couldn't I be taller?* A sudden epiphany occurred. I walked over to the boxes before picking one up and bringing it beneath the button. Slowly, I lifted myself onto the box careful not to break it. I once again tried to reach but still couldn't. I jumped down and took another box and stacked it on top of the first. I put the final box next to the first and climbed up. I leaped up and smashed my palm into the centre of the button. I smiled for a brief moment before falling onto the weak boxes. They gave way beneath me sending me plummeting to the floor. I landed hard letting out a small cry before sighing in relief.

However, I couldn't celebrate for long. I heard hissing sounds and saw a yellow gas rising from beneath me. I stumbled onto my feet. The gas was rising higher and higher with each passing second. I tried to get onto the boxes;forgetting they were broken. I climbed up and tripped into the box. I sat face first in the box as the gas surrounded me. I began to feel weary. My vision was becoming blurrier. I closed my eyes before inevitably passing out.

~

TEST SUBJECT 4 - Chanele.

I blinked my eyes open, my lids were heavy, willing for my vision to adjust to the new environment. As I looked around, it became apparent that I was in my child-hood bedroom, again. I was getting tired of this. However, this time it was different.

A deep, hellish voice came over from somewhere, it said, "The reason you are here is the reason you hate. Looks can kill, it is seen as fate. Your weight and appearance you must negate. The path to freedom is a reflection of life. The choice is yours."

*What kind of bad trip is this?* I noticed a tall, dark-haired guy stood by my bed. Was he there with me while I slept the whole time? And, where did the ominous voice come from? It sounded like it came from overhead, almost like a loudspeaker, not from him.

"Finally awake I see." He affirmed, matter-of-fact. There was nothing else to his tone, no hint that this was meant to be a jab at how long I'd been out for, or a statement of relief that I'd finally woken up. Just plainly stating a fact.

"Who are you? Why are you talking to be me?" I asked, annoyed by his presence. Who did he think he was, inviting himself into the house I grew up in and watching me sleep? When he didn't answer, I looked up at him to make sure I wasn't hallucinating, noticing the scar across his eye. Maybe this awkward situation could provide some entertainment.

"Are you sure I'm awake? Figured you couldn't tell left from right with that massive scar hindering your vision." That got a rise out of him. He inhaled sharply, his breath trembling as he exhaled in attempt to calm himself. It was funny how he let a snide remark from me get to him. I enjoyed it, the idea that I had enough influence over people for them to become frustrated over the smallest thing I said about them.

"Look, Chanele. I'm not here to engage in your childish banter or feed into your ego. Do you want to get out of here or not?"

"How do you know my name?" I was startled, but I tried not to let it show. No one had ever read between my lines this easily, especially not after I just made fun of them. "What do you mean 'get out of here?' Where exactly is 'here?'"

He sighed audibly. "What you need to know is that you were right about the food thing. You were smart for figuring that out, I won't deny that, even if your initial motive was rather vain."

"How is it vain of me to discipline myself in order to be beautiful?" I was genuinely confused, I didn't refuse food out of vanity, it was because I wanted self-control. I was better than everyone else who had to eat in order to function, I was above basic human needs. That's what I told myself.

"Never mind, I take it back. Your body's probably feeding off of your brain to prevent it from going into starvation mode. No wonder your so light, your head's practically empty." It was his turn to ridicule me now. I expected him to keep going, embarrass me even more, but he seemed to have something more important to say.

"If you want for all of this to stop, the nightmares, visions, glimpses of another world - you have to get out of here. To do that you must use the that mirror, " he gestured to a cloaked mirror in the corner, "and point out all of your insecurities; admit that you're not superior to everyone"

I couldn't believe what I was hearing. He was trying to tell me that I *wasn't* better than everyone. How could he? I was happy living in delusion. I was going to give him a piece of my mind, however, he was gone. /em Worst. Trip. Ever.

I sat on my bed, rethinking all the choices I'd made throughout my life that had led me to this moment, wondering what could've gone so wrong that a random man had enough audacity to imply I'm *ordinary.* The word felt like a slur, it left a bitter taste in my mouth despite not even saying it. I wasn't plain, normal. I couldn't be. Right?

Hesitating, I got up and wandered towards the mirror. *This is stupid. You shouldn't have to check to make sure that you're still perfect, you know you are. You don't have anything to prove to him.* No matter how hard I tried to convince myself though, a small part of me was still nagging me, telling her that I wasn't what I thought I was. I couldn't believe that my own conscience would betray me. As much as I loved to argue, doing it with myself was way less fun and much more stressful. Thinking so much made my pretty head hurt, and I was worried it'd give me premature wrinkles, but I couldn't stop. The thoughts were swirling in my mind, forming a tornado that destroyed any logic in its path.

When I arrived in front of the mirror the metaphorical storm grew more intense.

I couldn't bare to look at my reflection, not in this state. I was too on edge, too nervous, and I risked shattering the overtly confident, charismatic, grand persona I'd meticulously crafted to mask her insecure nature. Nonetheless, I had to prove to myself that I was still a cut above the rest, that I was worthy of respect and admiration (not that I needed it, the validation just helped to inflate my ego).

I took a deep breath and removed the cloth from the mirror. I stood for a brief moment, about to admire myself and revel in my victory at the fact that I'm just as gorgeous as I remembered, until I saw that my stomach stuck out as though I was pregnant. Was I bloated, or just getting fat? No, I couldn't be, I had hardly eaten anything the past few days. I hadn't even drank anything besides water and- oh god, *what were they putting in the water?* Were the drinks spiked too?

Unfortunately for me, whenever I notice something wrong with my appearance, more things start to show. My thighs jiggled, the fat hanging disgustingly off my leg bones. My nail-beds sucked, I had broad shoulders, and what was once an endearingly tiny waist was now a square, shapeless abdomen. My pristine figure seemed to morph into a wretched abomination, making a pathetic attempt at resembling something human. What was wrong with me, I had an incredible self-esteem just two seconds ago. How could looking at myself in the mirror affect her this much? Why was I so *sensitive?*

The bedroom door creaked open, re-

214

vealing a guard meant to escort me out of my pity-party. Humiliated, I followed without protest. Not only had I just ruthlessly criticised my image like the piteous, self-conscious people I detested, but I'd been caught doing it too. At least God gave his toughest battles to his prettiest soldiers - yes, that is how the saying goes - so I knew that someone still thought I was beautiful.

My vision began to blur and the hallway grew too stuffy. That yellow gas was back again. It smelt like a skunk took a dump in a dumpster and then dumped the dumpster-dump onto another smellier skunk. (Maybe I should switch aspirations from a model to a poet. What would be a moving way to describe the frustration and sheer exhaustion I was feeling?) I just

215

wanted to lie down on an airy cloud, so light that it would make me feel weightless, and drift into a peaceful sleep. Fighting my weariness felt like cognitive dissonance - I knew I was tired, but I knew I couldn't just fall asleep, again, especially in front of this guard who'd just caught my in the midst of my misery. I wouldn't succumb to the comforting promise of dozing into unconsciousness just to avoid dealing with these unfortunate circumstances, I was stronger than that.

*Mentally.* Physically though... I should've eaten more. It would've prevented my body from betraying me so easily when I shut my eyes.

# Chapter 27

# Level Three: Abuse and Loneliness

TEST SUBJECT 5 - Connor.

I awoke, I was in a familiar place, a living room. The TV was on and it suddenly cut to a creepy doll in what looked to be a cellar room. The doll spoke, "Hello Connor, I have been expecting you. The power of persuasion is key in life, say if you want to be a politician or wanting a certain piece in a song in a band. Your fiend of a father should walk in any second and he is not particularly content. Do what you can to survive and persuade. Any wrong choice will lead to you staying here for however long necessary. The choice is yours."

Five seconds later, my hellish devil of a father strolled in, looking like a drunk man off on a half-term break. He started talking about the life connection known as marriage. He suddenly blurted out, "Connor, son, you will marry this woman I have chosen for you." I thought for a few minutes, shaken by his father yelling like a person frozen in glacier ice.

"No dad, I won't, over my dead body." I could feel the tension building between us - our blood pressures rising by the minute. My father took a deep breath to prevent him from sending a fist in my direction and knocking me out or him throwing a spare brick at me. He replied almost instantaneously and watched as he said, "Well, either you will or you don't have a house." I thought, *seriously? Just because I won't do something that I have a right to deny, he slanders me for something that sounds like it came from patriarchal times.* I replied to my father, "Listen dad, I don't want to marry this random woman you decided to pick off the street for me, to be honest, I like this one girl in my uni."

It took a few minutes for a reply but he burst out with, "I don't care whoever this girl is, you are marrying this woman and that's final." I'm tried to come up with an excuse or at least a bit of help of some sort of push. I could say how the girl at uni is smart and is aiming to get a really high paid job. No, that wouldn't work, the guy's too broke and dense to possibly think of any amount of money. I could talk about her 10/10 looks. No, that wouldn't work because all he knew about mum is that he said she was a five and he made a joke once that two fives equal a ten but I disagreed and wandered off.

As I spoke, the tension built like a face-off between John Cena and The Rock in WWE. "Dad, trust me, the girl I like is probably ten through twenty times better than your beast of a woman." His fists started to clench, his voiced raised but also lowered to a war-ish tone and slammed his fists on the table in tantrum. As soon as that happened, I froze. My words started stumbling, my blood started to run cold. My heart starting pumping dark wine through my veins and sharpened all my senses. My breathes starting sounding like a gale. "You have failed, Connor, " the speaker returned, " You have failed to persuade your stubborn father to let you go out with a different lass."

~

TEST SUBJECT 6 - Paige.

I awoke in a gloomy forest, leaves covered trees up top twenty feet high. I was surrounded by thousands of Oak, Elm and Birch trees towering like skyscrapers. An audio tape rolled next to me as soon as I awoke. It disclosed, "The forest is a symbol of fear and mystery. Vision is limited and most times to none, you are alone. Overcome your agitation and you too can escape. You have ten minutes. Escape or stay. The choice is yours." As soon as the announcement finished, a ticking sound started. The person actually meant it. What do I do? As well as the tick of a timer, I could hear distant animal noises; the howl of a wolf and the hoot of an owl or pigeon. However, still I can hear the clamorous tick. *TICK. TOCK. TICK. TOCK.*

I questioned for a bit and decided to go to the animals' direction, or whatever creatures are there for that matter.

As I got closer to the animal noise, the further I could feel from freedom. The more I walked on, the less I heard the cries of the animals. I hate the feeling of loneliness, that's why I want to be popular and have a lot of friends at university, that's why I will be a author, to project my thoughts and not feel alone in this world. Suddenly, out of nowhere, a loud female voice echoed around, " *Five minutes left.*" I thought to myself, five minutes have gone! It's only felt like a few seconds.

"*Last minute.*" I still couldn't find the animals, what the hell? A few seconds later, I could feel my breath go short, feeling like I'm hyperventilating. I could feel a weird tingling sensation all over my body. I was trapped. My throat started to feel as dry as a desert. Out of the blue, my vision started to appear as if I was a fish. The last thing I heard was a buzzer sound and a person marching up to me.

# Chapter 28

# Level Four: Darkness, Death and Divorce

TEST SUBJECT 7 - Simsie.

I woke up in a pitch black room, as if
my eyes were shut but I knew I was awake.
Through the corner of the room, words resonated through the darkness.

A male, confident voice came from there
and declared, "There are no shortcuts in
life. Sometimes there is no light at the
end of the tunnel. The teeth of a preda-
tor hangs up high, kept a ring until they
die, say hi to hell and your freedom will be
applied. The choice is yours."

I'd say the room was approximately 50
metres long by 50 metres wide by 5 metres tall. As I pondered around, hands
flailing about to see if I could touch any-

thing, I noticed a rumbling sound; as if one of the walls were moving closer. Closer. After a poor observation, I came to the conclusion that there were spikes attached to the end of the wall. The walls themselves only moved around 1 cm ever 10 seconds. Suddenly, I remembered the resonation. 'Teeth' as in the teeth of a key and ring as most keys are connected on a ring. What did he say? Look high and then towards hell was your escape?

After what felt like 5 minutes, I found it. The golden shimmer of the key even though there was practically no light in the room. The texture of the key was as if it has just been bought. Now I had found the key all I needed was to find a lock. Luckily while on my way there I stumbled upon a texture that felt like oak, I knew it 'hi to hell' was the hint to the lock. I was sure it was back the way I came from. Eventually, I found what looked to be a trapdoor leading downwards. I put the clean key in the rusted lock; the squeaking parts scraping the side of my ears. I twisted the key once it was fully in and boom. I was out. WHAT THE HELL WAS THIS ALL ABOUT?

As I started to explore the damp trapdoor entrance, I smelt a coiling, acidic smell, creeping right into the crevices of my nostrils and down to the tunnels of my lungs. It made my head reel, spinning slowly before coming to a standstill point. Then I passed out, the taste of the poisoned air as sweet as a lullaby in my mind.

~

TEST SUBJECT 8 - Miss Lancaster.

I found a tape recorder on a box. I played it and a familiar sound reverberated. It uttered, "To escape a nightmare in real life, you sometimes need to lose that what you love the dearest. Live or die, Lancaster. The choice is yours." As I heard those last words, I felt a freezing chill sprint down my spine. What do you mean live or die? Can I actually die because of this? I focused on the tape recorder's words for a while then turned around to see a bunch of poor looking children - there skin was pale, their eyes were bloodshot and their eyes themselves were drooping as if it was a plastic bag on a hook just dangling.

Out of nowhere, I could feel a tingling sensation at the back of my brain telling me to do something about it. "Yeah, that seems like the right thing to do, " I whispered to myself. I rummaged around my pocket to see if I could give them anything but to my surprise there was actually one last pill in my pocket that I use if I ever have a headache from teaching. I crushed it up and gave it to the poorest one almost looking like they were on the brink of death. As I continued, I could see a sense of relief from the young child. Suddenly, out of the blue, the same voice on the speaker returned. "What a silly and foolish mistake you have made. Your consequences will be serious from your transgressions. You have failed" it said.

~

TEST SUBJECT 9 - Will.

I woke up in a dark spruce cabin, wood pieces were rotting in certain locations. In the corner of the room there was a TV, a remote sat impatiently on a glass coffee table. I turned and noticed on the sofa, there she was, Kara, my fiance. I sighed deeply as she politely said "Come, sit with me." I got agitated. I groaned, reluctantly, I went and sat with her. The TV flickered on and a puppet appeared, a quite horrifying puppet with a deep black mullet and a head that looked like a skull. At first it was facing sideways, suddenly it turned to face me and Kara and an audio tape played, syncing to the puppet's mouth. A demonic voice spread through the air particles, "The key to your freedom involves that what you love. Two brainpower for a price of one's freedom. Next to you is Kara, You should know and trust her dearly. Use your intelligence as a way to escape and maybe earn your freedom or stay in this fantasy world. The choice is yours."

I really didn't want to work with Kara but I wanted my freedom back. I smiled and began talking to break the silence, "Come on then, help, I want to get out."

"Oh my god fine, Jesus, " she groaned. She reluctantly got up and helped. We walked round the cabin, it looked like the front door needed a key.

"Find a key please, look in the other rooms. I'll look in here, " I ordered to my fiance.

"Okay Will." Finally, she left my side. I searched round, I checked every book, every shelf, every draw. Still found nothing.

"Anything?" I yelled to Kara as I began walking to the room she was in. She didn't respond, so I went in to find her sitting on the bed. "You're not even looking! Why? What the hell Kara?"

"Oh sorry, I didn't think it was necessary, " she continued, "I mean, I found a key but I don't know what it's for."

"You found the key? Why didn't you say?" I asked, walking to take it from her.

"No. You can't have this until you tell me the truth. Why do you hate me? You don't seem interested anymore, I want my Will back, the one that originally fell in love with me" she asked, I felt guilt but the truth is I just didn't love her anymore it's not the same from when we were younger. The spark faded.

"Fine, I'll tell you, just please, give me

the key. I will get my freedom, " I continued,

"I just don't love you the same anymore, I'm sorry, "

"She smiled, that's all I wanted to hear.
Thank you." She passed me the key and
we walked off to the door, I turned the key.
It clicked, I turned the handle and finally,
*freedom.*

# Chapter 29

# Game Over

The delicate sound of a soothing bell

ricocheted off of Miss Lancaster's crowded walls, flooding into her ears. Her eyes opened and she reached over from her bed onto her scratched, antique bedside table that was painted a faint carmine. Scrunched notes cluttered the surface, along with a tall pile of books - ranging from a variety of genres - and a coffee mug filled with chrysanthemums. On the table lay a vintage alarm clock which Miss Lancaster silenced. 6:45.

Laying in her bed, Sheila's eyes scanned the walls enclosing her. Her pupils gazed over countless pieces of paper, all covered with Jacobean poetry (the sheets that she actually thought were semi-decent) and pinned to the wall. She knew she had to do more but couldn't find the motivation. So instead she decided she was going to have a bath. Waking up early had plenty of benefits!

In her bathroom, she turned the gold taps attached to the porcelain bath that lay against the far wall and watched it begin to fill. Sheila always had a routine: run bath, pick a bath-bomb, get her towel ready and pick out her clothes for the day. She never failed to complete the routine, and if she did her whole day would be ruined.

After she had finished, she wrapped her soft towel around her small body and walked over to her large bathroom mirror. After letting it dry, she curled her pale, blonde hair and put on some light makeup, clasping her necklace around her neck and placing her bracelets on her wrists. Finally, she did her last step of her routine and put on her black, square glasses. 8:30.

Miss Lancaster felt relaxed, she had decided that she would admire the view from her arched window in the centre of her room. Her eyes roamed the garden and hovered over the large bed of roses, the section of the yard that was scattered with tulips, and where students tended to weeds and overgrown bushes.

Through the middle of the garden lay a well-trodden walkway that curved and winded along the patterns of the ground. At the far end of the garden, a vast forest opened up, inviting the people of the campus to explore and adventure through the many paths it held. 9:00.

The alarm went off.

DRING.

DRING.

DRING.

Sheila grasped the handles of her tote bag. It was filled will pens, pencils, and supplies she would need for the day and of course - her laptop.

~

A sliver of sunlight streamed into Paige's dorm through her dirty and weathered window, past the break between her intricate curtains and over her sleeping face. The warmth of the rays awoke her from her dream and her eyes flickered open. Paige turned over in her soft fabric blankets, tapped her phone and looked at the time displayed on the screen. 8:14.

She stumbled into her shared bathroom, rubbing her eyes from the lack of sleep she got, and started to run a warm shower. She prepared a fluffy towel for afterwards and put it on the bathroom radiator to warm. After her shower, Paige walked back into her room. She made her way over to her dark, hardwood wardrobe and removed a thick, patterned dress, perfect for the early September weather, off of the wooden hanger and put it on. The wide variety of shades ranging from deep pinks and vibrant oranges looked elegant against her natural dark locks.

Sitting down at her desk, Paige shoved pieces of paper filled with drafts off her work onto her soft, carpeted floor. With the new space, she brushed her fine, brunette hair and started to apply makeup onto her soft, doll-like skin. 9:00.

DRING.

DRING.

DRING.

It was time. Harsh, continuous sirens
filled the narrow dorm corridors. Everyone
started to file out of their small rooms -
filled with hunger and impatience - ready
to make the journey down to cafeteria like
they had done for the past few days, and
so did Paige. She joined into one of the
rows that spread across the lengths of the
long halls and made her way, in unison,
with the people surrounding her.

~

DRING.
DRING.
DRING.

The echo of an alarm filled Connor's
room as he opened his eyes. He sat up
in his small bed, decorated with blue covers and soft pillows, and looked across the

room at a small clock hung from a plain beige wall. 9:00. He had slept in again. *I'm going to be late*, he thought. His palms formed a thick sweat and his forehead soon became drenched. *What if I'm late?*. Now he was really panicking.

Connor ran past the large pile of painted canvases (half of them he had ruled as 'scraps') that lay in the middle of the room, the stacks of paint pots that hadn't been washed properly and tubs of paint brushes still dry and crusted from old paint. Once he had made it past these obstacles, Connor walked over to his wardrobe. He grasped the small, white door handles, flung open the doors and rummaged through his small pile of options. From a hanger he grabbed a red t-shirt, that he wore a lot, and from a drawer grasped some classic blue jeans.

He threw a piece of gum into his mouth to hide the fact he hadn't brushed his teeth and started to walk out of the door, joining the row of students on their journey to breakfast, making his way, in unison, with the people surrounding him.

# Chapter 30

# And The
# Winners Are...

Chanele awoke in a tattered, dark room. She looked around; the tall ceilings and wide walls trapped her with her thoughts. Chanele looked down at her body, noticing the gown she was in. It looked like something from an old asylum. She muttered under her breath, "Where am I?". She scooted off her bed and noticed it was one from a hospital. It had bloody sheets screwed up on it, they were dirty and old. On the pillow, a large, dull stain was soaking into the deep layers of comfort. As Chanele walked over to the other beds, she realised she recognised a few of the limp bodies unconsciously laying unaware of where they were. One was the server, from his body draped a long pattered gown, similar to Chanele's. She heard a groan

246

and spun her head in the direction of the noise. Nothing was there other than four other beds across the room. On them lay a few of her friends, or ex-friends. She walked towards them, noticing the mouldy patches on the walls surrounding her; the walls were also full of cobwebs and cracks. She scurried back to her bed, scared for what would come next.

Finally, the others started waking up, one by one.

"Where are we?" Someone asked.

"I don't think anyone knows, " Alan replied in a tired voice. They stood up and began to talk to each other. "Hang on, who's here?", Alan asks, his throat still irritated from the gas. Craig, Simsie, Chanele, Mickey and Will all responded, their voices weak and wavering

.

"So what should we do?"

Chanele replies "I think we should wait."

"Wait? Wait for what? Christmas?" Mickey forcefully responds, a (poor)sense of sarcasm still in his tone. Some of them began arguing and getting furious, they'd been cooped up for so long, they wanted their lives back.

"SILENCE!" a deep voice yelled, echoing loudly through the walls. Craig jumped out of his skin at the sound, he flung himself at Alan's arms, practically screaming. Alan chuckled at Craig as he held him in his arms. The others began talking "What was that?"

"I don't know. Just do what he said and shut up." Chanele said rudely, fed up of everyone.

"YOU HAVE PASSED, YOUR INDIS-CRETIONS HAVE BEEN LIFTED. PL-EASE LEAVE THIS ROOM NOW. YOU HAVE OFFICIALLY EARNED YOUR F-REEDOM" The voice appeared again, everyone listened carefully, they wanted to get out, but they didn't know how. Will looked around, there was a large sliding door on the far wall.

"This way guys." he said. The group followed him.

Simsie pointed at a small black lever and said, "Guys look! A lever, maybe we can get out if we pull it."

There was a struggle, but they all worked together and pulled the stiff, cold and rusted lever down. "WELL DONE." They heard as the sliding door slowly slid open. Craig looked at everyone, with a worried expres-

sion plastered on his face. Simsie stared
in awe. Alan stepped through the door,
the rest followed close behind, hoping for
them all to not get separated again.

"Ohh."

# Chapter 31

# The Last Lecture

They came out into what appeared to

be an office. It had all the things that an office should need: a bookcase swarming with monotonous books and articles, a desk overflowing with papers and various amounts of stationery, and collections of plants teeming in every single corner of the room. But it was different. The books had blank covers and spines of all different shades of white, the desk was a blinding white colour and had what seemed to be millions and millions of papers with a red stamp print reading 'classified' over them, and many plant pots in the room which were occupied with white hibiscus. Almost everything in the office was a certain shade of white. Dr Diffshire was sat behind the desk in an intricately detailed, antique and ghost-white armchair. But she was different. Not extremely different, but still dissimilar to her usual appearance. Her clothes were the same, but slightly baggier. Her hair was no longer blonde, smooth and waist length, but was now dark brown, coarse and shoulder length. She had an abundancy of freckles upon her face, a long nose, dull brown eyes (the colour of mud) and a scar across her throat.

"Come, sit down, " she said, her voice laced with an eerie calmness, as she gestured towards a worn down, cream-coloured sofa that could fit up to seven people.

"You must all be very confused, " she said with an awkward smile. Blank faces stared back at her like ghostsparted from their graves. "Firstly, I would like to congratulate you all for passing the tests! Not many of our patients succeed, especially not so quickly. So, we didn't expect many of you, really, " still, no one spoke. "It would probably be better for me to explain everything, wouldn't it?". Everyone began to nod slowly in agreement.

Dr Diffshire adjusted her position so that she was sat at the edge of the chair. "Right, " she mumbled. Then, after clearing her throat, "This is Somnium Asylum, the name might sound familiar to you. Many years ago, there was an apocalypse which not only ruined the wildlife and vegetation in the world, but also caused most people to develop mental illnesses and disorders based upon their past experiences. You were either sent here by your relatives or you were forced to come here by what was left of the government, to help you recover."

The patients were still bewildered, to them it felt as though their brains would never properly process this. "This used to be a university from the 13th century all the way over to the 21st century, when the apocalypse hit and it was abandoned. After that, I was hired by the government to restore it and convert it into an institution that would help the world come back to a state of somewhat normality. Alongside this, we have developed a drug here titled 'Enigma', which transports the user's mind into a state of dreaming. This state can be manipulated from the outside by us. The drug was put in all of your meals, so I hope that explains the unusual mood surrounding food. Overall, everything that you have been through, everything that goes on within this establishment, was designed to aid the recovery of the human race!" she smiled and added "And it is showing promising results."

"Well, there is one more thing that needs to be mentioned, but before that, any questions?" Her inquiry was met by heads shaking and a few timid replies of 'no'. "Good. Now, since you have been taking the drug for quite a significant amount of time, there will be a few... miniscule side-effects. But they, fingers crossed, shouldn't have any noteworthy modifications to your lifestyles, so you mustn't worry too much." She broke off for a moment to reach into a small compartment located in the desk and retrieved a pile of leaflets. "But if anything does happen that may be 'out of the ordinary', here is some information on what you should do. If the leaflet tells you to go see a doctor, come straight back to us."

Gingerly, she stood up and emerged from behind her desk. "I will now escort you to the exit, where you will be met by a small fleet of taxis. These taxis will drive you all to a hotel, where we will be able to monitor part of your recovery for a week or so. But do not worry, you will be reunited with your relatives soon, ". She strode over to the door, her heels clicking momentarily against the bare, wooden floor. "Follow me, " she said, stepping through the doorway. Some patients started to follow, some stayed where they were. Could they trust Dr Diffshire? Was this another one of her twisted experiments? They weren't sure. Yet, after a moment or two, the rest started to follow. They didn't want to separate themselves from the others, in case something strange occured.

All the corridors were the same identical, vivid white walls. The same off-white floorboards. No windows, just vents. It was a perfect prison. As the party moved onward, each footstep in sync with the other, the wooden floor-panels croaked melodically, like an orchestra of elderly frogs.

Finally, they arrived at the exit.

"So, this is where we part...for now, " Dr Diffshire remarked "You are free to go, ". She motioned to the doors with her hand, which opened instantly. The patients progressed ahead, Diffshire awkwardly shaking hands with each of them as they passed her.

But then they stopped.

Were they ready for this? Could they manage to survive in the real world? They didn't know.

But it was now or never.

They all stepped out in unison, each of their bodies consumed by the ethereal light of day.

Dr Diffshire watched them for a moment, wondering what it might feel like to finally be free, to finally get out, to finally experience a reality you didn't remembered as clearly as before.

She turned away, still pondering upon the matter, and stepped through a door. Through the door, you could see a small glimpse of another world. The university. Dr Diffshire's hair lightened as she exited the student's sight, becoming the Dr Diffshire of their fantasy world.

# Chapter 32

# One Year Later

Will:

"WEEEEEEEEEE!" Mark erupted into screams of joy as Will pushed him higher and higher on his new swing, wind brushing onto both of their faces.

Even though it was the anniversary of Will leaving Kara, his ex-fiancee and mother of his child, he was determined to make today a happy occasion. For Mark's sake over his. Even if he had to parent solo, it would be worth it, as long as he was happy. Maybe when the time was right, he could find someone else to love. However, right now, nothing mattered more than spending time with his child.

hanele has an eating disorder still)(also she loves herself but no to the narcissistic extent)(also she still wears designer clothes)(she's so silly :3)

Chanele:

In Beverly Hills, Chanele was in the bathroom getting ready for one of her boyfriend's black-tie events as his plus-one. She sprayed her Chateau Marmont 'eau de parfum, ' a welcomed change from the 'eau de toilette' she used to enchant her clothes with before she could afford nicer luxuries. She wore a strapless, floor length blue velvet dress, with a complementary white satin ribbon in her hair. Softer than said satin, however, was the gentle light from her vanity mirror, illuminating her face as she put on her make-up.

Many things had changed since since she'd been released from the asylum, not just the scents she preferred. She was going out with a guy now. Of course, the first thing she noticed about him was his opulence and charisma. However, after exchanging words over drinks and a messy morning-after with him one weekend, she started to think that there was more she could like about him than just the superficial things. He treated her like a princess, and he was wise, witty. Onlookers gave them weird glances as they strolled the streets - he was a little bit older - she didn't care though, she loved him. Maybe it was puppy love, but she's a dog girl, she can't help it.

She kept her lips red for him to seem like cherries in the spring, whereas before she wore baby pink chapstick. She let her hair down more often - she only put it up in extravagant styles to seek validation from strangers, but she doesn't do that anymore. She learnt that she can't be in the centre of attention as often as she'd like. That was fine, her boyfriend stole the spotlight half the time and Chanele was more than eager to flatter him.

One thing that stayed the same, however, was that she didn't get better to get happier or healthier because she *didn't* get better. Those thoughts were still there, lingering like the smell of coffee on her breath in the morning. Every time she dolled herself up she felt like she looked stupid, trying too hard like the kid who doesn't know they're being bullied. Every time she cried she felt like she looked stupid too, complaining like the privileged girl who's unhappy that she finally climbed up a tax bracket after landing a modelling contract. It all felt stupid; the way she tried to make sense of it, articulate it - the way she tried to diminish and ridicule it.

It's not like she didn't want to recover, she tried *so hard* to improve herself, but even if she did get better, the best she could be is still just another version of herself. That wasn't good enough. She couldn't keep lying, saying that she was going to change. She had nothing to show for the life she'd lived and there was no one who was better off for having known her.

Chanele sighed. There was no point in beating herself down, not now, not with a party she had to attend. Opening the small bathroom window, she took in the smell of flowers, still in bloom from morning showers, and readjusted her dress. She looked... nice. The blue hues of her garments complemented the velvet night, and she wondered if her old friends ever felt like this: grappling with their conscience in the way one grapples with a wet bar of soap in the shower.

Simsie:

In 'La Tasse a Cafe', a well-dressed customer entered, taking in the welcoming smells of coffee and fresh pastries. Simsie Brown greeted him with a warm smile before taking in his order.

"Un grand cafe au lait, s'il vous plait." The customer adjusted his tie whilst making his order.

"Tout de suite, monsieur!" Simsie started to brew his coffee. She loved her job, the smells, the sights, the tastes. Her cafe was finally getting the recognition it deserved and she was being flooded with good reviews and customers.

Even if being a tennis champion was only true in her fantasy world, she still oc-

casionally picked up a racket, just to test
it. It felt amazing to be able to do things
for fun, not just for the validation of others. Maybe her brief escapade to Somnium
'University' wasn't all bad.

The coffee was finished, and she served
it to her regular, waving him goodbye as
he left. She looked at the display of sweet
pastries in her window, wrapped up tightly
in baby-pink parchment. A young child
marvelled at the treats, begging his poor
mother for one. Simsie smiled, filled with
pride knowing that she was making others
happy.

Mickey:

The sliding doors of the recording stu-
dio shot open as Mickey eagerly walked
through them. Although a year had passed,
it felt like yesterday that he was still trapped

in Somnium and under the influence of Enigma. However, the fantasy was not all bad. He learned more about his guitar and song writing passions, which lead to him release 3 albums.

He looked around excitedly. The city was beautiful. With skyscrapers touching the clouds and people running and kids playing, he took a deep breath before looking down at himself. Dressed in a fancy suit, he was holding his guitar. He thought to himself, *you've made it Mickey* before giving the world a warm smile. He was wandering over to his car, before being stopped briefly by a young child.

"Are you Mickey Griffiths?" The young boy asked excitedly. Mickey nodded with a slight grin. He watched the boy jump around happily, before handing Mickey a piece of paper.

"Please can I have your autograph?" The kid said nervously.

"Of course!" Mickey said as he took a pen out of his pocket. He quickly signed then paper before handing it back to the boy.

"Thank you!" The kid exclaimed quickly running off to his parents. Mickey smiled to the boy before getting into his car and slamming the door shut. Almost immediately, he drove off before getting a call from his manager.

"Hello?" Mickey said as he answered the phone.

"Sir, you've got a concert in a week. We need you here now!" The voice said over the phone.

"What for?" Mickey asked.

"We need to know what you think on some last minute changes to the stage arrangements."

"Was that all?" Mickey replied.

"No sir, unfortunately one of the side acts are unable to make it to the show." His manager said in a worried tone.

"Okay I'll be there tomorrow, " Mickey said, trying to hide his obvious anxiety.

"See you soon Mickey." The woman said before hanging up. Mickey sighed to himself, rolled down his window and sped off into the distant horizon.

Craig and Alan:

It was a beautiful summer day. A single altar stood in a field of newly-grown flowers. Craig and Alan walked down the aisle together, staring each other in the eyes. A range of vibrant colours, from red and orange to blue and purple, filled their view. Hand in hand, they admired the beautiful surroundings. Doug and Smudge followed behind, wearing matching tuxedos, although Smudge's tuxedo barely fit around him. In a sunset sky, they walked towards the altar. After exchanging heartfelt vows, Craig gifted Alan with a bouquet of tulips.

"My favourite! You remembered!" Alan smiled.

"Of course I did!" Craig chuckled.

He placed a ring of daisies tied together on Alan's finger. Alan laughed and placed one on Craig's . A daisy chain - it was better than a ring for them - it had more meaning.

"You may now kiss the groom!" the vicar announced, smiling.

Doug and Smudge came running towards them and jumped up with excitement, causing Alan to tumble over. They laughed, loud, hearty laughs that echoed through the whole garden. This was it. This was their fantasy.

Dr Diffshire:

Sunlight spewed out of the windows and drowned the contents of Dr Diffshire's office in its paradisaical glow. The many awards and prestigious notices that hung on her wall reflected the light, like mirrors reflecting a dazzling image. She was still working as head of Somnium Asylum/vice chancellor of Somnium University, but had also won a Nobel Prize for her astounding developments in the medicine industry and life-changing discoveries in the study of neuroscience. She was happy. She had everything she wanted. Everything but a family. But she liked it that way...

John:

Although I still do hate the idea of sitting at a screen for 12 hours a day precisely typing away coding and protocols, I suppose I've gotten used to it by now. I still make the tests for new patients that qualify to leave the fantasy world. Even though I've been working on Project Somnium for over a year, I still find the fantasy world intimidating - an escape in reality - a shard in space and time only mad people can go.

My job is to stop mishaps from happening again. The tests are now more easy for the people who have snapped out and at least have some sort of intelligence - they have a larger chance to escape. My pay

is now raised to put up with the materi-
als for the test and technological supplies,
now up to 90, 000 a year. I suppose I am
rather satisfied with my life, even though
my neck still hurts quite badly.

Printed in Great Britain
by Amazon